His words sent a shiver down her spine.

"Duke…" she started, but he wasn't done.

"I respect your need for privacy, but I won't pretend like this—us—is just casual. Not to the world, and definitely not to you."

Anise swallowed. He'd never been shy about what he wanted, but hearing it said so plainly, with no room for misinterpretation, made her heart race.

"I just need time," she said, barely above a whisper.

Duke exhaled. "Time for what? To convince yourself you don't want the same things?"

"It's not that simple," she murmured.

"It is for me." His voice was calm but firm. "I love you, Anise."

Her breath caught. He'd said it before, but tonight, it felt heavier. More real.

"I won't force you to say it back," Duke continued, "but I need you to know—no matter how long it takes, I'm not going anywhere."

Anise closed her eyes, her grip tightening on the phone.

She wanted to believe that.

She needed to.

She was more damaged than she thought. What was stopping her from saying the words? What was preventing her from fully committing to Duke?

TRIED AND TRUE

BRENDA BARRETT

ALSO BY BRENDA BARRETT

FULL CIRCLE
NEW BEGINNINGS
THE PREACHER AND THE PROSTITUTE
AFTER THE END
THE EMPTY HAMMOCK
THE PULL OF FREEDOM
REBOUND SERIES
THREE RIVERS SERIES
NEW SONG SERIES
BANCROFT SERIES
MAGNOLIA SISTERS SERIES
SCARLETT SERIES
WILEY BROTHERS SERIES
PRYCE SISTERS SERIES
THE JACKSONS SERIES
CRIMSON HILL SERIES
SPICE AND STONE SERIES
RIDGEVIEW SERIES

ABOUT THE AUTHOR

Brenda Barrett is an award-winning and bestselling author who has a passion for writing real Jamaican romances.

When she's not weaving words that transport readers to exotic locales, you can find her nurturing her green thumb in the garden or doting on her beloved cats.

With an infectious zest for life, this author brings a unique perspective to her writing that is both relatable and thought-provoking.

Don't be surprised if you find yourself lost in the pages of her latest work, as she seamlessly blends romance with some drama, mystery, and suspense, or even sci-fi, leaving readers wanting more.

You can connect with Brenda online at:
Brenalbar.com
Twitter.com/AuthorWriterBB
Facebook.com/AuthorBrendaBarrett

Chapter One

Anise sat in the monthly Spice and Stone Division meeting, vaguely listening as her nephew, Leo Greystone, the head of the division, droned on and on about the launch party for their newest wine, Bay Rock. It was their first vegan wine and Leo's brainchild—he was dating a strict vegan who refused to touch their ordinary wines.

Leo was so excited about the finished product he could burst. Anise sat on the opposite side of the conference table as he ran through the virtues of the wine and its taste. So far, however, he had yet to address the actual plans for the launch—the very reason she was there and why he had urged her to attend.

Her title at Greystone Wines was Wine Exploration Director. This honorary position allowed her to dabble in wine development without the burden of actual responsibility. She wasn't trained in winemaking, nor did she pretend to be, but she had an instinct for flavors and a deep appreciation for the art of it all. Most of the time she simply enjoyed showing up for tastings, making a few dramatic pronouncements about what worked and what didn't, and then retreating to her life outside the winery—managing her beauty supply shop.

Today, however, Leo had been adamant that she attend.

"Your opinion matters, Anise," he had said, flashing that Greystone charm that usually got him whatever he wanted.

She shifted in her chair and crossed her legs, letting her gaze drift to the glass of Bay Rock in front of her. Deep ruby red, color was inviting, almost sensual. She lifted it, swirling the wine with an expert flick of her wrist before bringing it to her nose. The aroma was pleasant, had a bright fruity flavor with a hint of earthiness. She took a sip, letting it linger on her tongue.

Not bad. Surprisingly smooth.

Leo paused mid-sentence, watching her expectantly. The room had gone silent. Anise set the glass down deliberately, pressing her lips together in thought. She could practically hear Leo's heartbeat from across the table.

"It's good," she said finally. "I can't tell the difference between this and our other wines. And I love the name Bay Rock."

Leo smiled. "That's a relief. We intend to name all the vegan lines with 'Rock' at the end, like a series. However, we'll only move ahead when we see how well this does on the market."

"Can we move on to the launch party aspect of the meeting?" Anise asked impatiently. "I have a thing somewhere else."

"As usual, Anise. I know your skin starts to itch if our meetings run even a smidge over fifteen minutes," Leo said with a smirk.

Everyone chuckled. They knew her by now. If they wanted

to keep Anise's attention, they had to give her bullet points and no frills.

"It's a side effect of my ADHD," she said. "You all know that. Now, get to it."

"Okay, moving on," Leo said quickly. "I was thinking of a romance theme for the launch."

"Perfect," Milly, one of the marketing execs, said. "When I first tasted Bay Rock, romance came to mind. Not to mention, it's red, and Valentine's Day is six weeks away."

"We could do a Valentine's launch," Leo nodded. "That was at the back of my mind—make it a grand celebration of love. We could have DJ Duke headline for us."

"That alone will sell the tickets," Milly said. "But six weeks is short notice to book the hottest singer on the airwaves. That song of his, It's Always You, is all I hear on the radio. Getting him to perform live could be impossible."

Leo shook his head. "I would agree with you, but we have a secret weapon." He peered down the table at Anise.

Anise shifted in her chair. She didn't know what Leo was getting at, but she didn't like how he grinned at her suggestively—like he knew something. Her relationship with Duke Jones was a secret. As far as the world knew, she was single and unattached. And she liked it that way. Her life these days was peaceful and free of press intrusion.

"What are you talking about?" she asked, clearing her throat.

"This." Leo pointed to a magazine. "The headline reads, Are They Together or Not? The writer says, 'This is the third event where I've spotted DJ Duke and Anise Crystal hanging out together. Are they an item? Watch this space.'"

Anise rolled her eyes. "Rubbish. I hang out with people, and they always write about it."

"The picture tells a story, though," Leo mused. "Duke is

looking at you with unconcealed adoration."

"Let me see that," Anise grunted.

Leo passed the magazine down the table. It moved slowly—everyone wanted a look.

When she finally got it, she sighed. The picture was taken a week ago at their mutual friend's birthday party when Duke gave her an ultimatum.

"I'm tired of us hiding, Anise. Something's got to give. I'm tired of being on the outside of your life, looking in. I want to shout it from the mountaintops—I don't care who knows."

But she cared. She didn't want to let the public in. Or her family. Or anybody else, for that matter. She wanted to keep this relationship from prying eyes and outside opinions, because, for the first time in her life, she was hopelessly and stupendously in love.

"Anise," Leo prompted. "Since you are allegedly close to DJ Duke, in whatever capacity, can you ask him to perform for us on Valentine's Day at our Bay Rock launch?"

Anise looked up at Leo. "Of course, I'll ask him."

"So, are you two dating?" Milly asked eagerly.

Anise leveled Milly with a look, her expression unreadable. "What does that have to do with the launch party?" she asked coolly, taking another sip of her wine.

Milly grinned but backed off. "Just curious."

Leo, however, wasn't letting it go that easily. "You didn't deny it," he sing-songed, tapping his fingers on the table.

Anise sighed, setting the glass down with more force than necessary. "I said I'd ask him, didn't I?"

That was all they were going to get out of her. She wasn't about to confirm or deny anything—not in a room full of people, not when she and Duke were still trying to figure things out. He was ready to tell the world. She wasn't. He wanted marriage and children. She was a mother of three and a grandmother of two and felt she had already done all that.

And that was the problem.

Leo, satisfied for now, clapped his hands. "Alright, moving on. We'll finalize the venue and guest list this week. Milly, start working on a promo strategy. If Duke agrees, we'll build a campaign around that."

The meeting wrapped up quickly after that, much to Anise's relief. As everyone shuffled out, Leo caught up with her at the door.

"You know," he said, lowering his voice, "if you really love him, you can't keep him in the shadows forever."

Anise stiffened. "I don't—"

Leo held up a hand. "Not my business. But just think about it." He patted her shoulder before walking away, leaving her standing there, her stomach twisting.

****

"I need to ask you something," she texted Duke as soon as she sat in her car. The day was remarkably cool and windy. It was the first week of January; luckily, she had worn pants. Her loose, silky top was almost whipped over her head—she had forgotten to wear a bra, as usual. Luckily, no one was lurking in the Greystone Wines parking lot to see the show.

"I need to ask you something, too," he texted back. "I'm at my father's shop. Want to swing by?"

"No," Anise texted. "I'll wait for you at my place this evening. I have lunch with Jada."

She started the car and debated which route to take to Jada's place. She should cancel, but she promised her friend she would visit. Jada's father had died a few months before.

He had left all of his worldly possessions—including the house she was living in and running her business out of—to Jada's estranged husband. Jada felt betrayed and confused.

Her husband, whom she had stopped speaking to two years ago, was now her landlord. It was too much.

Fathers could be so unnecessarily cruel to their children, Anise thought darkly. She suspected that Jada's father thought that it was a good idea to force her to talk to her husband, but it was a ham-handed way of doing things and completely uncalled for. What if Jada's husband was cruel and kicked her out of the house she had grown up in, the place that was both her residence and her business?

Anise would watch how everything unfolded keenly. She wasn't about to let one of her closest friends go homeless. She was already thinking of solutions. Jada could operate out of her Constant Spring shop. She had recently opened a beauty supply store in that area, and the shop was huge. She could make some space for Jada's designs. Her friend made custom outfits; having her business in a beauty supply store was a stretch, but hair, makeup, and fashion went hand in hand.

She had met Jada seven years ago at a magazine shoot. Jada had designed all the pieces for the shoot, and Anise had taken one look at them and fallen in love. Jada's aesthetic was sleek yet bold, effortlessly blending timeless elegance with a modern edge. Her designs were the kind of pieces that made a statement without trying too hard—much like Jada herself.

Anise smiled at the memory as she pulled out of the parking lot. Jada had a sharp wit and a no-nonsense attitude, but beneath that exterior was someone deeply passionate about her craft. They had clicked immediately, even though they were a good fifteen years apart in age. At times, Jada felt like the more mature one.

She exhaled slowly, gripping the steering wheel as she merged into traffic.

Jada's situation weighed on her mind. How did a father justify leaving everything to a man his daughter hadn't spoken to in years? Did he believe this was some grand plan to fix their broken marriage, or had he simply preferred Jada's husband over his daughter? The thought made her stomach turn.

Anise didn't believe in suffering through bad relationships for sentimentality. If it was over, it was over.

She turned on the radio to her favorite talk show, Claire Talk; her friend Claire Manderson usually had some interesting guests and dealt with intriguing topics. Anise had been on her program more than ten times. At this point, they should name the program Claire and Anise Talk. Anise chuckled to herself.

The sound of Claire's voice filled the car, smooth and familiar. "Welcome back to Claire Talk, where we dive deep into the topics that matter and sometimes the ones you never expected to be talking about. Today, I've got a very special guest, a woman who's been through the ups and downs of life, love, and career, and she's here to share her story. Stay tuned for some real talk about relationships, boundaries, and finding the strength to move forward, no matter the obstacles."

Anise smiled, settling back into her seat. It was going to be her kind of show.

Chapter Two

Jada's place was in a cute little residential community off Norbrook Drive, where she ran her dressmaking business from her garage. The split-level abode was painted a cheerful shade of coral with white trim, and lush bougainvillea climbed the front trellis, softening the modern lines of the house. Anise pulled into the driveway, giving herself a moment to mentally prepare before stepping out.

Jada must have been watching for her because the front door swung open before Anise locked her car.

"Girl, you are right on time," Jada called, her voice tinged with exhaustion and relief. She looked good as usual—her caramel-toned skin glowed, and her hair was styled in a curly mohawk.

They exchanged a quick hug before stepping inside. Jada led her straight to the kitchen, where she had laid out a spread.

"It's takeout from Bud and Sally's," Jada said. "I was in the mood for Italian. I hope that's good. I got your favorites—carbonara and chicken marsala."

Anise nodded. "That's perfect."

"Richard called," Jada said as she sat down. "I had to take the call because, obviously, he is holding all the cards, and he dropped a bombshell on me today."

"Oh really?" Anise raised her eyebrows. "What did he say?"

"He wants me to move to Montego Bay so that we can give our relationship a fighting chance. He claims he doesn't want to use my home and business as a bargaining chip—he just wants a chance for us to make a go of it. And if we don't work out, he'll sign the place back over to me, no questions asked."

"That's… reasonable," Anise said, serving herself some food. "More than I expected, to be honest. I was prepared for us to fight him with all guns blazing."

"I don't want to try again." Jada snorted. "Have you forgotten why I left him in the first place?"

Anise frowned. "The letters from his ex… and the fact that you lost the baby."

"That, and he didn't love me," Jada said. "He married me because of my father's investment in his business. I was the starry-eyed, naïve, infatuated fool who thought he was genuinely into me when all he wanted was my father's money."

"Oh boy," Anise murmured. "I still think you jumped to that conclusion."

"He didn't love me. He was still telling his ex that he loved her," Jada hissed. "And that he wished they were still together."

"But that was what she said he said," Anise replied exasperatedly. "Listen, I am not one for defending men.

They are, for the most part, sneaky little devils, but you never got Richard to explain himself."

"All I want," Jada said, ignoring Anise, "is a man who will love me for me. I want something like what you and Duke have. He loves you—flaws and all, inside and out. That man wears his emotions for you on his sleeve. To me, you guys are relationship goals."

"Oh, goodness," Anise murmured. "I can't recall ever being someone's relationship ideal before. You're probably the first person who has used me as someone to aspire to. I need a moment for this to sink in. It's a strange feeling."

Jada chuckled. "I love everything about you guys. I mean, you two are as open with each other as it's possible to be—no secrets, no unnecessary drama, no games, no power struggles. Just two people who genuinely enjoy each other's company and make things work. That's what I want."

Anise twirled her fork in her carbonara, trying to process Jada's words. She and Duke were solid, but did they have it all figured out? If they did, why had she been so apprehensive about the two of them lately? He wanted marriage and children. She did not.

"Maybe you're giving us too much credit," Anise said, taking a bite of her food. "We have our moments. I am a forty-two-year-old grandmother who is comfortable with her life. He is a thirty-five-year-old famous divorcé who wants marriage and children. I am slowly coming to realize that we may be incompatible after all."

Jada waved her off. "You two are compatible. Those things are not dealbreakers. In my case, I don't understand why Richard wants us to try again when he never wanted me in the first place." She sighed and leaned back in her chair. "I should just tell him no and be done with it."

"I think you should give him a second chance and really

listen to his side of the story next time," Anise said. "To his credit, he hasn't been with his ex in the two years you were apart."

Jada scoffed. "Not that we know of. He could be seeing her in secret."

Anise shrugged. "Maybe, maybe not. But why hasn't he divorced you if he was so desperate to be with her? Why hasn't he moved on?"

Jada frowned and stabbed at her pasta. "Guilt. Obligation. Maybe he feels bad that I lost the baby, and this is his way of making amends."

"That's possible," Anise admitted. "But, Jada, you have to admit this is a pretty extreme way to ease his guilt. He didn't just give you money or apologize and move on. He wants you to move to Montego Bay to be close to him. That's not a casual request."

Jada sighed, rubbing her temples. "I don't know, Anise. I just can't shake the feeling that it's all about control. My father controlled me my whole life. And now, through this house and business, Richard has the power to do the same."

Anise reached across the table and squeezed her friend's hand. "I get it. And maybe that's true. But if you don't at least hear him out, you'll never really know. What if he actually means what he says? What if he genuinely wants to fix things?"

Jada exhaled slowly, her expression unreadable. "I'll think about it."

"Good." Anise leaned back, taking another bite of her food. "And in the meantime, just know that if you decide to walk away, you'll land on your feet. You always do."

Jada smiled faintly. "I hope you're right."

A comfortable silence settled between them as they ate.

After a few minutes, Jada set down her fork and smirked.

"Enough about me. Let's get back to you and Duke. You really think you two are incompatible?"

Anise hesitated, then sighed. "I don't know. Maybe I'm overthinking things. But sometimes I wonder if we were meant to have different futures."

Jada gave her a knowing look. "If you really believed that, why are you still with him? You are Anise Crystal, the woman who gives no second chances and who moves on at the drop of a hat. If you are not feeling the vibe, out the door you go. Trust me when I tell you this, Anise. Your futures are not misaligned if you are still with him."

****

Jada's question ran through her mind as Anise drove home. She took a moment to chew on it. Why was she still with Duke? In the past, she had no problem ending relationships when they no longer served her. This one was different.

Duke wasn't just another man she dated for fun or companionship. He had become a part of her life in ways she hadn't expected. He challenged her, made her laugh, and somehow, despite their differences, he made her feel seen.

Maybe that was why she hadn't walked away.

Still, she couldn't ignore the gnawing uncertainty at the back of her mind. He wanted things she had long since decided weren't for her at this point in her life. It wasn't fair to him was it—staying in a relationship when their end goals didn't align?

Anise sighed as she turned into the Wilde Building parking lot. She had moved into the luxury residential complex a year ago after buying an apartment for a song from her brother, Nelson Greystone.

He had been forced to sell it because his wife, Devina Shae, didn't want him to have a private apartment to disappear to whenever they had disagreements.

Duke had helped her move in. He lived in one of the six penthouse suites in the same building. They were practically neighbors—she lived just a floor below him. They had even exchanged keys. It was a symbolic gesture in their relationship and the furthest she had gone with any man. Sharing keys was serious. It meant trust, it meant access, and maybe permanence.

She slid into her assigned parking space and turned off the ignition, her fingers lingering on the key. Her mind drifted back to the first time she met Duke, back when she would have never imagined they'd get this far.

Chapter Three

Three Years Ago

Anise adjusted the neckline of her wrap dress and checked her reflection in the mirrored wall of the rooftop bar. The Kingston skyline stretched behind her, the city twinkling under the evening lights.

She was here for the launch of Jaxon Wilde's dream villas, set along a hundred miles of St. Mary's coastline. It was an investor's party, and she had decided to invest in Jax's latest venture because his previous ones had been wildly successful. He was her son-in-law—married to her daughter, Cinnamon, and father to her precious grandson, Valerian Jett, aka VJ. Investing in this project felt like investing in VJ's future, too.

A few Greystones were milling around. Nelson Greystone was there with his wife, Jaxon's mother, Devina Shae—the former model turned perfumer, who had named her latest perfume Sweet Jett in honor of their mutual grandson.

The super-rich world was small and insular. Anise, who had recently inherited a fortune from her late father, Richard Greystone, was only beginning to understand what it truly meant to be part of the serious money class.

She had seen glimpses of it before while dating a few men in this economic bracket, but she had always been an observer, never a player at the table. Now, she had a seat at the table and it was heady business.

"Mom," Cinnamon said behind her. "You look awesome!"

Anise spun around. "You don't have to sound so surprised about it."

"I mean," Cinnamon chuckled, "you're not wearing any wigs or weaves, and you have on light makeup. Your hair is longer than I've ever seen it. You look gorgeous. Like, seriously gorgeous. My goodness."

Anise grinned. "Thank you. I must say, you're not looking bad yourself."

Anise looked Cinnamon over. Her firstborn looked exactly like her. They could have been twins. They shared the same rich, dark brown complexion that gleamed under the bar's soft lighting, and sparkling, almond-shaped eyes that held a playful, confident gleam. Cinnamon had full lips, a delicate nose, and a youthful, doll-like face framed by a mane of dark curls that fell to her shoulders.

Cinnamon was wearing a sleek, form-fitting dress in a deep green shade that complemented her complexion and highlighted her figure. Her hair was styled in loose waves, and her makeup was bold yet effortless, emphasizing her high cheekbones and glowing skin.

"How is it that your hair is much longer than mine?" Cinnamon frowned.

"My wigs," Anise shrugged. "They give me a chance to tuck my hair away for months, and your sister comes to my place every two weeks to care for my real hair. She's the one to thank for my flourishing mane."

Cinnamon chuckled. "Cayenne is my hairdresser too. I will tell her I want exactly what she's using on you."

Anise laughed. "It gives me a certain thrill when the younger ones are envious."

"You're not that much older than me," Cinnamon snorted. "But you're right—I am envious."

Anise chuckled. "Where's VJ? Is he here in the building?"

"Yes, with his nanny and sound asleep." Cinnamon frowned. "We'll be staying here all week, so you can check in on him tomorrow. Come early—all the grandparents are here."

"Including his grandfather, Darren Wilde? Jax's actor father?"

"Yup." Cinnamon nodded. "He's an investor too. He's over there talking to DJ Duke." She pointed toward the open bar.

Anise turned and stared. She was going to tease Cinnamon and say, wouldn't it be nice if he were single?

But instead, her eyes connected with DJ Duke—aka Duke Jones—and it felt as if the room stilled. No joke. She had heard people describe eyes connecting across a room in those terms; she had just never experienced it.

She had difficulty dragging her eyes away from Duke's.

"He's handsome, isn't he?" Cinnamon chuckled.

"I guess," Anise murmured.

"You guess?" Cinnamon whispered. "Mom, you need glasses if your response is I guess."

"Which one of them are we talking about?" Anise said faintly. Her heart was doing a weird gliding-pounding motion.

"DJ Duke," Cinnamon said. "He's staring at you. He's

coming over. I guess this is where I say bye, see you tomorrow. I can feel the sparks flying between you two from here."

"Wait a minute." Anise gripped Cinnamon's hand. "Isn't he still married?"

"Nope," Cinnamon said. "I heard his divorce was finalized just this week."

"What's he doing here?" Anise hissed. "Is he going to sing?"

"He's an investor," Cinnamon said. "He has shares in Wilde Property Development from its inception—he was one of Jax's first investors. They're friends from college. Singing is just one of the things Duke does. He owns one of the six penthouses in the building. The man is probably as rich as you. According to Jax, Duke has been building his investment portfolio since high school. His mother is Yvette Jones, the stockbroker, of the program Money Schmoney Honey. I guess she taught him a thing or two."

"How old is he?" Anise asked.

"Thirty-two," Cinnamon said. "Just seven years younger than you. Not bad, in my opinion."

"Why are you playing matchmaker?" Anise asked.

"I'm not." Cinnamon grinned. "Jax mentioned that he went to Duke's place to welcome him back to Jamaica. He was staying in England with his cousin, Jairo Jones, to hide away from the media furor surrounding Madge Whitlock and the murders."

"Sad business. It hits differently when the person you thought you knew—and were married to—ends up being a criminal," Anise muttered. "I would hide away, too. When it happened to me—when good-for-nothing Paul Aubry tried it with Cayenne and Sage—I did hide away with Grandma Saidie, not daring to show my face."

"You guys have a few things in common," Cinnamon nodded. "When Duke came back home, he was watching Claire Talk in the penthouse resident lounge, and they had you on."

"I wonder which interview it was?" Anise murmured.

"Who knows?" Cinnamon grunted. "You're always on Claire's show, spilling your business and sharing your opinions."

"Not lately," Anise said. "I'm cutting back on being so open. My last show was about my charity; we're working to combat child sex abuse on a community level."

"Maybe that's the one," Cinnamon nodded. "He was avidly staring at the television and telling Jax that he wanted to meet you. Of course, Jax told him you were his mother-in-law. He was excited about the connection."

"You don't say," Anise whispered. "Maybe he wants to contribute to my charity."

"Or maybe he just wants to meet you," Cinnamon murmured. "You are, quite frankly, gorgeous—aging like fine wine. That gives me hope, since I have your face."

Anise smiled. "What am I going to say to him?"

"You're refreshingly honest and blunt. Maybe he could use a friend like you. Or more than just a friend—who knows?"

Anise inhaled deeply, her mind racing as her gaze flickered back to DJ Duke, who was now making his way toward them. The way his confident stride matched the quiet intensity in his eyes was impossible to ignore.

Her heart did a strange flip in her chest, and for a moment, she felt like a teenager again—unsure of what to do with this unexpected attention.

She looked at Cinnamon, who was watching her with an almost mischievous grin.

"You're not helping," Anise muttered, her voice laced with amusement and mild frustration.

Cinnamon laughed softly. "I'm just saying, Mom, you deserve someone who can handle your fire. And from what I've heard about Duke, he's been through the wringer. The two of you should have some interesting conversations at least. Maybe you can cheer him up; he has had a tough go of things lately."

Anise couldn't help but let out a small laugh at her daughter's enthusiasm. "I'm not some kind of... fixer, Cinnamon. I don't go around trying to 'cheer up' people. But, I guess a little friendly conversation never hurt."

"Exactly!" Cinnamon whispered as she gave her mother a playful push toward Duke. "Just be yourself, Mom. You're a force. He'll either be intrigued or keep walking."

Anise rolled her eyes but couldn't deny that part of her felt the pull. There was something about DJ Duke—something both intense and disarming. Maybe it was the way his energy seemed to fill the space when he entered a room, or the subtle vulnerability in his expression, a shadow of pain mixed with hope.

By the time Duke reached her after stopping to talk briefly with a few people who had commandeered his attention, Anise's heart had calmed down just enough for her to regain her composure. She looked up at him, meeting his gaze with a steady, knowing smile.

"DJ Duke, I presume?" she said, her voice smooth and warm, though her pulse betrayed her with a quick, nervous beat.

"Well, it's actually Duke Jones—or Duke," he smiled. "And you are Anise Crystal, right?"

"Right," she nodded. "Anise Crystal Cooper. Though, like you, I tend to drop the last name for the public."

"I thought you would have changed your name to Greystone," Duke said. "I was at the launch of your namesake wine, The Anise Crystal, and saw Richard Greystone's message to the family. I thought you would have fully embraced the Greystone bit of your name. He made it clear in his video that you were a member of the family and should be treated as such."

"He did, didn't he?" Anise smiled. "I can't recall seeing you perform that night."

"Before I could perform," Duke said, "someone was kind enough to show me the breaking news about my wife being an accomplice in some pretty heinous crimes. I was numb after that."

"Oh yes, that was the night, wasn't it?" Anise murmured.

Duke nodded. "I thought it was all a mistake. Then I went home and saw the letter she left me admitting everything. I was gutted. It's hard to believe that was over a year ago. I fell apart for a while but think I'm better now. I'm officially single, and I heard you were, too."

Anise looked at him. He was refreshingly honest. It was a little unexpected. "You asked about me?"

"I sure did," Duke nodded. "I've always been a little fascinated by you. I watched that interview you gave about your childhood—how you were molested by who you thought was your father and then ended up married to a molester yourself. You weren't afraid to reveal your dirty laundry. So many families sweep their dirty laundry under the carpet and silently suffer. Madge did it, and look where it got her."

"Thirty years to life," Anise whispered.

"I like how bold you are," Duke looked at her admiringly. "You take a no-holds-barred approach to life. You live out loud. I'd love to get to know you better, if you don't mind."

Anise tilted her head slightly, considering his words. There was no hesitation in his voice, no attempt to dance around the subject or soften his interest. He was direct and confident—but not in an overbearing way. And she appreciated that.

"You'd love to get to know me better?" she repeated, arching a brow. "That's a line I haven't heard in a while."

Duke chuckled, his deep voice sending a shiver down her spine. "I don't do lines," he said smoothly. "But I do believe in being upfront. I think we'd have a lot to talk about."

Anise exhaled slowly. This was not where she'd expected the night to go. She'd come here to support Jax, to make an appearance, maybe sip a glass of wine, and leave before things got too boring. Now, she was standing in front of DJ Duke—Duke Jones—who was looking at her like he truly saw her.

"Maybe we would," she admitted, her voice softer now.

His lips quirked. "Then let me get you a drink. Or… do you prefer to make a quick exit once your duties are done?"

Anise hesitated. Her instinct was to retreat. She wasn't the type to linger at events longer than necessary. And yet, something about the way Duke looked at her made her want to stay just a little longer.

She glanced at Cinnamon, who was pretending not to eavesdrop but was watching them like a hawk. Then, with a small smirk, Anise met Duke's eyes again.

"A soft drink," she agreed. "Just one. I have ADHD, and I am on medication."

Duke nodded, unfazed. "Got it. No alcohol. What do you like?"

"Ginger ale," she said after a beat.

"Good choice," he replied, signaling to the bartender. "I'll take one too."

Anise folded her arms, studying him. "You don't drink either?"

"Not tonight," he said easily. "I like to keep my head clear. I've been staying away from things that could impair my judgment. I had a rough couple of months when I used to drink myself to sleep."

She considered that. He was being refreshingly honest. Most men didn't admit their vulnerabilities so soon after meeting, especially when trying to impress someone. But Duke wasn't trying too hard—he wasn't trying at all, really. And that was… interesting.

Their drinks arrived, and he handed hers over. "So," he said, leaning against the bar, "tell me something real, Anise. Something I won't hear from anyone else in this room."

She arched a brow, taking a sip. "You want real? From a woman you just met?"

"Why not?" His gaze was steady, patient. "You seem like someone who doesn't waste time on small talk."

She tapped her fingers against her glass, debating what to tell him. Then, with a tilt of her head, she said, "I don't actually like parties when I'm on medication. When I'm not, they're great—the rowdier, the better."

Duke grinned. "Wow, hearing someone talk about their disorder so frankly and openly is refreshing. What's it like with attention deficit hyperactivity disorder?"

"We are really going hard and heavy fast, aren't we?" Anise chuckled. "Usually, I work up to telling people that I talk a lot and jump from one topic to the other because that's the way my brain functions."

Duke nodded. "So what's it like?"

Anise studied him, searching for any trace of pity or condescension. She didn't see any—just curiosity. Genuine interest.

She exhaled, swirling the ice in her glass. "It's like always having ten browser tabs open in my brain. Some are playing music, some are buffering, and some keep reloading while I try to close them. And when I'm off my meds, it's like those tabs all start playing at full volume."

Duke let out a low whistle. "Sounds intense."

"It can be," she admitted. "But it's also why I thrive in chaos. Too much quiet, my mind bounces off the walls, searching for something to latch onto." She gave him a wry smile. "That's why I usually love parties. All the noise, the energy—it keeps my brain occupied. But on my meds? It's different. It slows things down and makes everything a little too sharp, too in focus. Which is great for work, but for fun?" She shrugged. "Not so much."

Duke nodded, taking that in. "So, you're here tonight because…?"

"Because I am a shareholder in this venture, like you, I suppose." She took another sip of her drink. "Jax is my son-in-law, and it sounds like a good project."

He chuckled. "I couldn't believe Jax was your son-in-law when they told me. You're what, two years older than he is?"

Anise chuckled. "Six, actually."

Duke leaned in slightly, his expression thoughtful. "So if you weren't on your meds tonight, would you be on the dance floor instead of standing here talking to me?"

Anise smirked. "Probably. Or I'd be trying to talk my way into the DJ booth."

His eyebrows lifted. "You mix?"

She shook her head. "Nope. But when I'm off my meds, I have all the confidence in the world. I'd convince myself I could."

Duke laughed, shaking his head. "Now that, I'd pay to

see."

Anise found herself smiling. This was nice. Easy. She wasn't used to men listening, asking real questions instead of waiting for their turn to talk.

"Alright, your turn," she said, setting her glass down. "Tell me something real, Duke. Something I won't hear from anyone else in this room."

His smile faded slightly, but not in a bad way. He considered her for a long moment, then said, "I almost quit music a few years ago."

That surprised her. "Seriously?"

"Yeah." He leaned against the bar, his fingers tapping lightly against the glass. "Got burned out. Lost my love for it. Was this close to walking away." He pinched his fingers together.

"What stopped you?"

He met her gaze. "A conversation. With someone who reminded me why I started in the first place."

Anise tilted her head. "Must've been a hell of a conversation."

Duke's lips quirked. "Yeah. It was."

She narrowed her eyes slightly. "Are you going to tell me who it was?"

He took a slow sip of his drink, then set it down. "Maybe if you stick around a little longer."

"Come on," Anise urged, "tell me. Of course, I am sticking around. You are refreshingly interesting."

"It was Chex Hastings, my best friend, producer, and brother from another mother. He said, 'Do one more song,' and that song was 'No Promises.' It blew up."

"I loved it!" Anise said, "Still playing it, to be honest. In the city lights where shadows dance, whispers in the wind taking a chance. Walking down the street, lost in reverie. No promises tonight, just you and me."

Duke smiled. "Chex was the one who wrote it, and I find it ironic while singing it, simply because I am a guy who is big on promises. I'm not heavily into transient relationships; one-night stands are not my thing."

Anise gasped. "Mine neither."

"Good." Duke nodded. "So how does having ADHD affect your relationships? Is there anything I should know, look out for, or prepare myself to handle?"

Anise blinked, caught off guard by the question. Most people didn't ask things like that—not this early. They usually figured it out the hard way.

She set her drink down, studying him. "You really want to know?"

Duke held her gaze, steady and sure. "Yeah. I do."

Anise exhaled, tapping her fingers against the bar. "Alright. Well, for starters, I can be… intense. When I'm interested in someone, I get hyper-focused. It's like my brain latches onto them, and suddenly, they're all I think about. But then, just as quickly, my focus can shift—and I am just not that into them anymore. I can't seem to keep a relationship to save my life. I take some getting used to, and I guess nobody so far thinks I'm worth the effort, and I certainly haven't made an effort with anyone either."

Duke nodded. "Got it. What else?"

She tilted her head, watching him carefully. "I interrupt a lot. Not because I'm not listening—actually, it's the opposite. My brain connects ideas so fast that if I don't say something right away, I'll lose it."

Duke's lips twitched. "I noticed."

Anise huffed a laugh. "And I forget things. Important things, sometimes. Not because I don't care, but because my thoughts are constantly moving at a hundred miles per hour. I might need reminders for dates, anniversaries, or even conversations we had two days ago."

Duke leaned on the bar, his expression thoughtful. "So, what helps?"

She hesitated, not used to someone wanting to accommodate her instead of expecting her to deal with it. She wondered if he really understood all of what she just told him.

"Patience," she admitted. "And understanding that I'm not flaky, I struggle with time management. Oh, and don't take it personally if I zone out mid-conversation. I also have problems regulating my emotions, which means I'll flare up if something displeases me about you and will probably ghost you after that."

Duke nodded again as if filing that information away. "Anything else?"

Anise raised an eyebrow. "You still interested after all that?"

Duke grinned. "Anise, I was interested before you even started talking. Now, I'm just better informed."

She shook her head, a reluctant smile tugging at her lips. "You're something else, Duke Jones."

He clinked his glass against hers. "So I've been told."

****

Anise snapped out of her recollection of their first meeting and got out of the car, stepping into the private parking garage of the building. The soft overhead lighting cast a glow on the polished concrete as she made her way to the elevator, the sharp click of her heels echoing in the otherwise silent space.

She swiped her keycard, and the sleek metal doors slid

open. Inside, she leaned against the mirrored wall, watching the numbers climb. Sixth floor. Home.

She would take a long shower, maybe pour a glass of wine, and then wait. Duke had said he wanted to ask her something, and from the way he sounded, it was serious. They had been together for three years—he wasn't usually so dramatic.

The elevator let out a soft chime as the doors opened to her floor. Plush carpeting muffled her steps as she walked to her spacious corner apartment with floor-to-ceiling windows overlooking the city skyline. At night, it was spectacular— the twinkling lights stretched for miles, and the sunsets were nice too. But now, it was the golden hour.

She kicked off her shoes and tossed her handbag onto the cream-colored sectional. The apartment was quiet, save for the distant hum of the AC. She headed straight for the en- suite bathroom, turning on the rain shower. Steam curled into the air as she stepped under the hot water, letting it ease the tension in her shoulders.

Her thoughts drifted back to Duke. What could be so important? He wasn't the kind of man to build up unnecessary suspense. If he wanted to talk, it meant something.

By the time she emerged from the bathroom, wrapped in a plush robe, her nerves had settled—mostly. She padded barefoot to the wine fridge, pulling out a bottle of red. She had barely taken her first sip when her phone buzzed.

She reached for it, glancing at the screen. It was Duke.

Anise hesitated for a moment before setting the glass down and unlocking her phone.

Are you home yet? He texted.

She exhaled slowly and typed back.

Yes, just got in.

She watched the three little dots appear, then disappear. A

moment passed before his reply came through.

I'll see you soon.

She stared at the message, her heartbeat a little unsteady.

Whatever this was, it wasn't small.

Chapter Four

It was a family business meeting and he had to be there. Whenever there was a decision to be made about JoJo's Barbershop, everyone, including him, had to be involved, even though he wasn't involved in the day-to-day operations.

His parents had arranged it that way. Both of them were business-minded. His father, John Jones, was a savvy entrepreneur who had built the barbershop from the ground up, and his mother, Yvette, was the one who handled the financial side of things. Together, they had created a successful, tight-knit business serving the community for over two decades.

Duke didn't mind the meetings—at least not most of the time. It was the obligation that came with being part of the family business that irked him. He wasn't the kind of person who liked to sit at a table discussing numbers and expansion plans. He preferred the creative freedom his music career gave him, but his parents had always insisted that the business was a family affair. They wanted him to take ownership, even if he didn't always share their passion for it.

They were finally expanding, after being in one location for years, they were opening another JoJo's in Montego Bay. His sister, Deanna, and her husband, Michael, would be in charge of the day-to-day operations of that one. They also had ideas about extending the space to include a gaming lounge and a bistro.

Deanna sat at the table, making notes and asking questions. His mother, Yvette, had her glasses perched on her nose, examining the figures like a dutiful accountant. Michael was nodding studiously at every point his father-in-law made. At the same time, Michael's sister, Alyssa, stared at Duke with a stony determination in her eyes.

Duke didn't understand Alyssa's role in the rollout of the new JoJo's—she was a real estate broker. In fact, she was the one who had found the location for them as soon as the listing had landed on her desk. Her work was done.

Shifting uneasily in his chair, he avoided her gaze. Lately, he had been steering clear of Alyssa at all costs. She had seen him at his absolute lowest a few years ago. It was the evening after going to court and hearing the testimonies against Madge. Alyssa had shown up at his apartment, ostensibly to cheer him up, dressed in an itty-bitty costume and acting like a femme fatale. His self-control had been in the dirt, and he had lost it. He had almost had sex with her. If his best friend, Chex Hastings, hadn't shown up at the moment of consummation, maybe he would have.

It would have been meaningless and regretful. Alyssa was practically his little sister. It would have felt incestuous. He couldn't imagine the consequences of actually going through with it. Their parents were friends; they had even coordinated school drop-offs and pick-ups, had joint birthday parties, and treated them like siblings.

There had even been expectations—well, vague hopes—that the Jones children would marry the Grant children one day and continue the family unity. That had worked out for Deanna and Michael; they had been inseparable since childhood. But Duke had never been attracted to Alyssa. She had always felt like a sister—an extension of Deanna. They were besties, and he had found them equally annoying growing up.

A long time ago, under pressure from his mother and Aunt Cassie, as he called Alyssa's mother, he had taken Alyssa to her senior dance. Her friends had loved it. By then, he had started making waves in the music business and was well known. But after the party, he dropped her home and went to another event.

Alyssa had been put out with him for years after that.

He remembered her yelling at him, What's wrong with me? Why can't you like me?

There was nothing physically wrong with her—she was undeniably pretty, tall, and statuesque, with curves in all the right places. But he had never felt the need to cross the line from friendship to romance, no matter how much their mothers willed it.

Then, seven years ago, he had seen her at a house party, being pawed at by some guy. He had stepped in, rescued her, and, from that night on, they had become real friends—not just two people forced together by their families. She had started hanging out with him and his crew, joining them on their adventures. She had become one of them.

And then he had met Madge, a dancer at Sensuous City, and had fallen for her instantly.

Everybody had loved Madge.

Except Alyssa.

After their first meeting, Alyssa had pulled him aside and said, "Duke, I have a vibe about her. She's not good for you."

He had scoffed at her. "Madge is perfect for me. She gets me. Why don't you like her? Are you jealous?"

"Get over yourself, Duke Jones. My crush on you crashed ages ago," Alyssa had said witheringly. "I know Madge's type. The fake hair, fake nails, fake breasts, fake eyelashes—women like that are usually covering up something. Why does she always wear a pound of makeup? And why does she always wear those wigs? Those tattoos of hers look like graffiti. Do you even know what her real hair is like?"

Duke had chuckled. "So your problem with Madge is that she's into fashion and loves to dress up? I don't care about her real hair or her love to dress up. She is a lovely person. I want to marry her."

"You can't turn a ho into a housewife," Alyssa had said waspishly. "And you can forget inviting me to your wedding. I will not endorse this madness with my presence."

"She's hiding something," Alyssa had said firmly. "And you're too caught up in her to see it."

Duke had brushed off her words. He was crazy about Madge—her wild energy, her confidence, the way she made him feel like the only man in the world for her. His attraction to Madge had been all-consuming. They had gotten married six weeks after meeting. They had stayed together for five years—until the revelations about her criminal past.

He had been burned. He was a one-woman man, like his dad, and he had thought she was his one. His parents were the best example of a good marriage that he knew. They had met when his mother walked into the shop and asked for a big chop. She had decided to go natural and wanted a skilled barber to do it for her.

His father had volunteered, then asked her out, and the rest was history—though it hadn't been smooth sailing. His mother came from a rich, conservative family that tended to look down on working-class people like his dad. They had protested the union, even going so far as to disinherit Yvette.

She hadn't cared. Together, she and his father had made the business work. With her business savvy, they expanded JoJo's Barbershop into the busiest barbershop in the city. Duke admired how his parents had fought against all odds—against societal expectations and family pressures—and built a successful, thriving business. Despite all the challenges, their love for each other was evident.

It was the kind of marriage Duke had hoped for with Madge.

He had always assumed they would tell their children how they met in a nightclub when he had been shooting a music video. She had been the star in Can't Get Enough of You, playing his love interest. The song was about lust at first sight.

And true to the song, he couldn't get enough of her. Even though they had felt an enormous pull toward each other, they hadn't consummated their relationship until their wedding night. Many people found that hard to believe because Madge had been a dancer at a nightclub who supplemented her income by sleeping with customers, and he was supposedly a playboy singer who had women flocking to him like flies. On paper, neither of them had seemed like the marrying kind.

He had thought he had it all figured out with Madge. They would get married, enjoy a few years of freedom, and then have at least two children—just like his parents' blueprint. But it hadn't worked out that way. Madge had neglected to tell him she already had two children—the ones he had thought were her younger siblings. And her third pregnancy, from the same family member who had raped her, had resulted in a botched abortion that left her infertile.

Duke thought darkly that he had never really known his wife.

The irony was that it wouldn't have fazed him if he had known about her children. He wouldn't have minded being a stepfather. He could have adjusted to not having kids of their own. It wouldn't have been a dealbreaker. He had loved her. He still had a soft spot for her even now, despite knowing how she had lied to him—about everything. Despite knowing that she had killed those women at the behest of her father, Leonard Crooks.

Even after the divorce, he hadn't completely written her off. He had his accountant send a monthly stipend to her mother, who was taking care of her children, and he still visited her in prison whenever his schedule allowed. She needed all the friends she could get on the outside. Prison life was awful without support. His contact at the penitentiary usually passed on her requests, and he supplied them as best as he could.

Their last conversation floated in his mind.

She had looked a little worse for wear during his visit. Her eyes had seemed bruised as if she had been in a fight, and she had lost an alarming amount of weight after a bad bout of flu.

"I look worse than I feel," she had greeted him in the recreation area. They were allowed face-to-face visits. "But you look great—better than when you were married to me."

Duke had smiled.

"I heard it's the Anise Crystal glow-up," Madge had said sadly. "You two are an item now."

"How'd you hear that?" Duke had asked.

"Pearl." Madge had fidgeted, looking down at her hands. "She keeps me up to date with all the current affairs. She visits me often. Though… not as much now, since she had the twins."

Pearl Day Hastings had been her best friend and should have been her last victim. Madge had opted not to poison Pearl as she had the other women her father had coerced her to murder. Pearl was quite thankful for that. So thankful that she was keeping up her friendship.

"Oh," Duke said out loud.

"I am well cared for in this place between you and her. It's more than I deserve." Madge's eyes teared up, and he looked away. He hated it when she cried. During his first couple of visits, after she was incarcerated, he swallowed his own tears and waited until he was in his car to let them loose.

He didn't feel tearful now, though. It seemed as if seeing her didn't elicit the same emotions it once did. He had truly gotten over her. And it was all because of Anise.

"Everyone has moved on," Madge whispered. "Pearl is happily married and has twins with Phillip. Chex found an ex-girlfriend who had his kid and is now married to her. Somehow, I can't picture Chex being married. Pearl said he's so happy these days, and he's actually sleeping at night. He's no longer into the nightlife."

Duke nodded. "Yep, that's what the world has come to. Believe it or not, Chex's wife's name is Garnet Silver. Does the name Silver ring a bell?"

"No." Madge shook her head.

"Well, her grandmother, Fern Silver, was your father's first victim. That's how he made his wealth. He married her for her money and then killed her, robbed her children of their inheritance, and used it to finance his empire."

"Can we not call Leonard Crooks my father?" Madge sighed. "Just call him Leonard Crooks."

"Why'd you do it?" Duke asked her for the first time. He couldn't believe he had never addressed this with her. She had written him a long letter outlining her secrets—how she was raped by her step-uncle between the ages of thirteen and fifteen, her botched abortion with her third pregnancy that had rendered her infertile, lying about her children and saying they were her brother and sister, and finding her real father, Leonard Crooks, who knew all her secrets and had used them to blackmail her into killing the women who dared to leave him by poisoning their champagne.

Yet, he had never asked her why she had done it. He had always asked why she hadn't come to him and been honest with him. She would have been unblackmailable after that, but she had put up a façade and allowed herself to be used.

"I did it because I didn't want to lose you or the life we had," Madge said. "I loved you beyond reason and had already started the lies. I couldn't stop. I didn't want anything to change. I didn't want you to treat me differently. I just…" She bit her lip and looked down at her hands. "I was an idiot."

That was the first time she had admitted it so plainly. Duke felt a pang of something—pity, maybe, but not the same raw hurt he had once carried. He had loved her, but love without trust had been doomed from the start.

"You didn't have to lie," he said finally, shaking his head. "You never had to lie."

Madge let out a bitter laugh, her fingers twisting together. "Easy for you to say now. But you are Duke Jones, the hottest DJ in the game, Mr. Untouchable. And I was… just me. The girl from the club with too many secrets and too much baggage. Besides, I had millions of followers on YouTube."

She exhaled sharply, her shoulders slumping. "I wanted to be perfect for you. For them. I wanted to be enough."

He stared at her, taking in the weight of her confession.

"You were enough," he said, surprising even himself with the sincerity in his voice. "Even with everything, Madge. If you had just been real with me... maybe things would have been different."

She looked away, blinking rapidly. "Maybe."

Silence stretched between them, filled with years of what-ifs and roads not taken. Duke felt the final thread of whatever had once bound them snap. There was nothing left here—just a woman he had once loved, now a shadow of herself.

He had Anise in his life now, a woman who was so real with him it sometimes hurt. There were no secrets with Anise. She had laid them all out for the world already, and she told him privately what she didn't tell the world.

His father was still speaking, snapping him back to the present.

"...and that is why I am so grateful that I have you children..."

Duke had missed the first part of the speech, but he knew what was said—something about the Jones legacy, passing on generational wealth, etc. His father always gave this speech during their business meetings.

He would probably never have children to make this same speech to. The thought made him a little sad. His one issue with Anise was that she wouldn't even meet him halfway on the topic.

"I have my kids already, Duke. I love babies but can't picture myself having any at this age."

And that was why he had been looking into surrogacy, discreetly inquiring about the process in Jamaica. It seemed like a fair compromise—he would get someone else to have his children. He was going to pitch the idea to Anise this evening, right after he asked her to move in with him at his new place in Ridgeview. Just a trial run to see how well they'd get on living together.

"You were spaced out during the entire meeting," Alyssa said, looking at him as the meeting wrapped up.

His parents were huddled together, staring at his mother's computer. Michael stood behind them, pointing at the screen. Deanna sat nearby, visibly counting something.

What had he missed?

Duke shrugged. "I have a lot on my mind."

"Does any of it have to do with this?" She pushed a brochure his way.

He saw that it was one of the surrogacy brochures from the fertility clinic—the same one he had flung into the passenger seat of his car.

"It fell out of your car. How many of them did you collect?" Alyssa asked.

"A bit," Duke sighed. So now his secret was out—and with Alyssa, of all people.

"I hope it works out for you," Alyssa said, without much interest. "I crashed your meeting today because I overheard Deanna and Michael discussing moving into your guest house at Ridgeview. However, they weren't sure if they should ask you since it wasn't close enough to work. Since they're dragging their feet, I thought I'd put in my request first."

"Oh my God, Alyssa," Deanna said, overhearing that bit of the conversation. "Talk about being underhanded."

"I need a place to stay for six weeks while I attend an in-house training program at my company's office in MoBay. It would be a long commute every day from Kingston to

MoBay. As soon as the course is done, I'll come back to Kingston. I won't be a long-term guest at your place, like Deanna and Michael would be," Alyssa said quickly. "Besides, I think they shouldn't be in your personal space, cramping your style."

Duke chuckled. "That's it?"

"Yes." Alyssa nodded.

"Wait a minute, big brother," Deanna said cajolingly. "We wouldn't be cramping your style. We'd just be staying until we find suitable accommodations of our own. We'd hardly be there anyway."

"You can all stay. It's a big place," Duke shrugged.

"Ooh!" Alyssa clapped her hands. "Thank you so much. I'm grateful enough to consider having your babies if you want. You won't have to use a surrogate."

Deanna's eyes widened. "What is she talking about?"

"I'll explain later. I have a long-overdue meeting with a friend—right about now."

He got up before Deanna or his parents could quiz him further. They had looked over when they heard the word babies.

Chapter Five

Anise was standing on the patio, staring at the city lights, when he let himself into her apartment. She was dressed in a long, floaty kaftan, and her hair was pulled into a curly topknot. He could smell her perfume from here—light, floral, sweet. It was so like her that his heart clenched. Would he ever get tired of this woman?

"Hey, sorry I took so long," he said as he walked over and hugged her from behind. "As it is, I spent most of the family meeting zoned out."

He kissed her neck, and she spun around to face him.

"What are you doing for Valentine's night?"

"Nothing," he said with a smile. "Are you planning something?"

"I hadn't thought that far ahead," Anise admitted, cupping his cheek. "I was in my monthly Greystone Wines meeting when, lo and behold, your name came up to perform. Leo wanted me to ask you. It's for a new vegan wine called Bay

Rock."

"I'll call my agent," Duke said. "She'll get in touch with Leo."

"Cool." Anise smiled. "So what is it that you wanted to ask me? You've been so dramatic about it."

Duke stared at her for a while. "How do you feel about surrogacy?"

Anise's smile faltered, and she pulled back slightly, studying his face. "Surrogacy?" she repeated, her tone cautious.

"Yeah," Duke said, watching her reaction carefully. "I know how you feel about having more kids yourself, and I respect that. But I still want to be a father." He exhaled, running a hand over his beard. "I've been looking into it. Discreetly."

Anise blinked a few times, then turned back toward the city lights. "And when were you planning to tell me?"

He sighed. "Now. I didn't want to bring it up until I had real information, but Anise… this is important to me."

She crossed her arms, her fingers drumming lightly against her forearm. "So let me get this straight. You've been researching surrogacy behind my back, and now you're just… presenting it like a done deal?"

"It's not a done deal," he said quickly. "I just wanted to talk to you about it. Get your thoughts. You said you can't picture yourself having another baby, and I hear you. But does that mean you can't picture me having one either?"

Anise let out a slow breath, tilting her head as if considering his words. "I don't know, Duke. It's not just about the pregnancy. A child is a lifetime commitment. Are you really ready for that?"

"I am," he said firmly. "I've been ready."

She turned to face him fully now, her dark eyes searching

his. "And if I say I can't do this? That I can't sign up to raise another child with you?"

His stomach tightened. He hadn't wanted to think about that possibility, but here it was, staring him in the face. "Then we figure it out," he said, his voice quieter now. "But I need you to be honest with me, Anise. Are you saying you don't want this at all? Or that you just need time?"

She hesitated, biting her lower lip. "I don't know," she admitted. "I love our life, Duke. I love us. But this? This changes things."

Duke nodded slowly. "I get it. I knew you'd say this. I guess I've been watching everyone around me being fathers, and I want in on it. Chex got his vasectomy reversed, and he's expecting a girl any day now with Garnet. Audra is also having Jairo's baby—also a girl. They're thinking of calling her Jai."

"Cute name." Anise turned away from him.

He read defensiveness in her posture.

"I wouldn't mind having a kid too," he admitted. "Today, my father was talking about legacy, and it hit me that I wouldn't have anybody to give that speech to. All your children are grown up and have families of their own. They don't even know that you and I are together because I am a secret."

Anise sighed. "Why do we always end up talking about this lately?"

"Because it's on my mind," Duke said, stepping beside her. "I don't want to lose you, but I don't want to be a secret anymore, Anise. I am the marrying kind of man. I want a family—however, that looks, whether by adoption or surrogacy. I spoke to a doctor at the clinic, and she said the process was straightforward. They could find a surrogate, use my sperm, and... in nine months, I could have a child of my own."

Anise closed her eyes briefly, her fingers tightening on the balcony railing. "And where do I fit into all of this, Duke?" she asked, her voice quieter now.

He reached for her hand, but she didn't turn to him. "With me," he said simply. "I don't want to do this without you, Nise. I love you. I see a future with you. But I also see myself as a father and don't want to give that up."

Anise exhaled sharply and finally turned to face him. Her expression was guarded, but he could see the conflict in her eyes.

"You say you don't want to lose me," she murmured. "But what if this is what pushes us apart?"

Duke's jaw clenched. "Then tell me now," he said, his voice rough with emotion. "If this is something you could never accept—if it means the end of us—then I need to know."

She didn't answer right away. Instead, she stepped closer, resting a hand on his chest, right over his heart. "I just need time," she whispered. "I need to sit with this. To understand what it means for us."

Duke covered her hand with his heart hammering beneath her palm. "Okay," he said, his voice steady despite the nerves swirling inside him. "Don't take too long, though. I'm ready for this."

She nodded, her gaze softening. "I'll sleep on it."

"Good," Duke said. "I have something else to ask."

"My goodness, what is it now?" Anise asked.

"Would you move to Ridgeview with me for a couple of months? I'll be working on an album at Knightsbridge Farm. Chex built a studio out there and expanded his brother's Airbnb offerings. He's inviting a couple of international stars to record, and I'll be on a few of the songs, but I'll be preempting all of that with an album of my own."

"That's great!" Anise said. "About the album. Not so great about the moving. I have a ton of things to do here in Kingston."

"Name one," Duke said, narrowing his eyes at her.

"I, er…" Anise bit her lip. "Give me a moment. I'll think of an airtight excuse."

Duke's expression darkened. "Anise, I'm getting tired of this. You don't travel with me, you don't interact with my friends or family, and you don't want us to be seen in any public space where anyone could guess we're together."

His voice sharpened. "What exactly are we doing here?" The frustration he'd been holding back spilled over.

Anise exhaled, turning away from him, but he wasn't letting her off that easily.

"Seriously, Nise. Are we just killing time? Am I just your secret escape when you feel like it? Because I'm done pretending this is enough for me."

Her shoulders stiffened. "It's not like that."

"Then what is it?" he challenged. "Because from where I'm standing, it looks like you want me in private but not in public. You want my love, but only behind closed doors. And now, when I ask you to come with me—to just be with me—you can't even come up with a reason why you won't."

She turned back, her eyes flashing. "You knew what this was, Duke. From the start."

"And I was fine with that—for a while." He ran a hand over his face, his pulse pounding. "But I can't keep doing this. I love you, but I won't be hidden. I won't be some well-kept secret you only acknowledge when convenient."

Anise's lips parted, but no words came out.

"Can you even say it?" Duke pushed. "That you love me?"

Her silence was answer enough.

Duke let out a hollow laugh, stepping back. "Got it." His chest felt tight, his stomach a knot of disappointment. "I'll be at Ridgeview. I'm leaving by the end of the week. If you decide you want more than this… you know where to find me."

And with that, he walked out, leaving Anise alone in the dim glow of the city lights.

Chapter Six

Instead of going to his penthouse after their argument, Duke went to the resident lounge on his floor. Every floor had one, but the penthouse lounge was exceptional.

It was stocked with Greystone Wines, even some rare ones—courtesy of Leo Greystone, he expected. He didn't keep liquor at his place, not since his scary descent into drunkenness after finding out about Madge. In fact, he hadn't had alcohol of any kind in months.

Tonight was an exception. He needed to take the edge off—he was nervous about him and Anise.

The tenth-floor lounge was quiet, the city lights sprawling beneath the floor-to-ceiling windows. Duke exhaled sharply, rolling his shoulders as he walked over to the sleek bar. He grabbed a bottle of Cinnamon Jade and poured himself a glass, watching the light green liquid in the dim light.

His conversation with Anise kept replaying in his head. He knew this would be an uphill battle.

He sat down in one of the plush chairs and closed his eyes. Whenever they had disagreements, he had to remind himself why he was with Anise in the first place.

He loved her and he knew what he was getting himself into. He had gone into this with his eyes wide open.

Now, he had to self-assess—was he even justified in being mad at her? She had always made it plain that she was fine with the way her life was. He was the one who had changed the status quo. He was the one who wanted more.

He was at a crossroads in their relationship. Should he stay or leave?

He could end it right now. The very thought gave him a pang.

It would just be between them—the only people who knew about them were their best friends, Chex and Jada and his cousin Jairo. As far as he knew, nobody else knew for sure. Their friends speculated, especially when they went to parties, but no one knew what was happening.

Their breakup wouldn't create waves. Anise would adjust in a few days and he would be free to be with someone who wanted to have his children and love him.

This nameless, faceless woman would be normal—unlike the two great loves of his life, Madge and Anise. And unlike Madge and Anise, she wouldn't have any baggage. He probably wouldn't love her as deeply as he did Anise, but that was the trade-off. He wouldn't feel as passionate, either, but it would be a nice change of pace from the emotional rollercoaster he'd been on for years.

Stability. Predictability.

A woman who would hold his hand in public without hesitation, who wouldn't flinch when cameras flashed, who wouldn't insist on keeping their love confined to the shadows.

He took a slow sip of the Cinnamon Jade, letting the warmth spread through his chest.

The idea of moving on should have felt like a relief.

It didn't.

His mind drifted back to Anise—her sharp wit, the way she challenged him, the fire in her eyes when she was arguing a point she refused to back down from. She could frustrate him like no one else, but she also made him feel alive.

Madge had done that too.

He certainly had a type.

Duke exhaled, tilting his head back against the chair.

Was he setting himself up for heartbreak all over again?

He had known it was a possibility after pursuing Anise for months on end while she thwarted him at every turn.

Sometime in the Past

"Did I tell you that I'm setting up a studio at Knightsbridge Farm?" Chex asked him.

They were in Chex's office at the studio. It was just a casual visit—Duke needed someone to talk him out of pursuing Anise Crystal. He had been on his way to see her but had stopped at the studio instead.

He didn't understand her. They had a good rapport for two months—she called him at odd hours and said whatever was on her mind. She even invited him over to her apartment three Sundays in a row. She cooked, they watched a movie and chatted some more. And then… nothing. She had ghosted him.

"I'll be recording cows and goats singing," Chex said, staring at him.

"My God, no." Duke looked at his friend askance. "Is that what Right Vibes Studio has come to?"

Chex chuckled. "Just checking to see if you were listening."

"Sorry, I wasn't listening. I came here to talk about a lady who is driving me crazy."

Chex leaned back in his chair. "Glad to hear you've moved on from Madge. How can I help?"

"Her name is Anise Crystal."

Chex whistled. "I know Anise. She's wild but fun—and incredibly pretty. A friend of mine dated her. He said she's not easy to tie down. He said something she didn't like, and she ghosted him—shut him down, cut him off. He thought she'd be easy, with all the news reports about the men she's dated, but he said she wasn't easy at all. So be warned."

"I know this," Duke murmured. "Anise is like a feral cat. But just like a cat, I find her cute, cuddly, and adorable, and I just want to pet her and feel her curled up next to me at night."

"Mmm." Chex nodded. "Let me do an internet search on how to tame a cat. You can adapt the results to Anise."

Duke laughed.

Chex grinned, typing dramatically on his keyboard. "Alright, let's see. Step one—gain their trust. Well, that's obvious. Step two—don't make sudden movements. Duke, are you scaring her off?"

Duke sighed, rubbing his hand over his face. "I don't know, man. One minute we're good—she's laughing, cooking for me, calling me at random hours to talk—and the next, she's ghosting me, like we were never a thing."

Chex nodded knowingly. "Classic cat behavior. They come to you on their terms. The moment you think you own them, they disappear under the couch for a week."

Duke groaned. "That's not helping."

Chex chuckled. "Okay, real talk. Anise is… complicated. She's not the settle-down type; you, my friend, are a relationship guy. She might not be the one if you're looking for something serious."

Duke shook his head. "It's not even about that. I'm not asking her to marry me. I just want her to stop pretending this thing between us doesn't exist. We have real chemistry—the air between us sizzles with it."

Chex studied him for a moment. "Have you told her that?"

Duke hesitated. "I shouldn't have to. She knows it."

"Anise is the kind of woman who will run the second she thinks she's being backed into a corner. You have to be patient with her. Or decide if this is worth the chase."

Duke exhaled, staring at the ceiling. "That's the thing. I don't know if it is. But I can't stop thinking about her."

Chex grinned. "Well, in that case, my best advice is… ignore the cat. She'll come back when she's ready."

Duke chuckled despite himself. "You and your metaphors. In case you weren't listening, she is ignoring me."

Chex leaned back, smirking. "No, she's not. She's testing you to see how committed you are. Don't be too eager, but don't disappear completely either. She likes the push and pull—it keeps things exciting for her. If you chase too hard, she'll bolt. If you back off completely, she'll think you never really wanted her in the first place."

Duke frowned. "So what, I play her game?"

Chex shook his head. "Nah, you play your own game, but with her rules in mind. Give her space, but stay present. Let her know you're there without making her feel trapped. And most importantly, don't let her think she's the only one calling the shots."

Duke leaned forward, elbows on his knees. "Easier said than done. I don't play games, Chex."

"Then don't," Chex said simply. "Be honest, but be smart. You're dealing with a woman who has spent her whole life avoiding attachment. If you want her, you have to show her that being with you won't cost her independence."

Duke nodded slowly. "So what do I do now?"

Chex grinned. "Go about your life. Let her feel your absence. If she wants you, she'll come looking."

Duke exhaled. He hated the idea of waiting, but maybe Chex was right. Anise wasn't like anyone he'd ever been with. If he wanted her in his life, he'd have to let her come to him on her own terms.

And God help him, he hoped she would.

She knocked on his door the following Sunday.

The knock was unexpected—usually, no one had access to his door unless it was one of the other five residents on the penthouse floor. But Anise visited Jax and Cinnamon regularly, especially since they had the baby. He had just come out of the shower, a towel wrapped around his waist.

Anise looked him up and down when he yanked the door open and wetted her lips.

"I was just in the neighborhood and thought I would say hi."

He stepped aside for her to pass. "Would you like to come in?"

She stood as if rooted at the door. "Maybe I shouldn't. You look edible. I've been celibate for two years."

Duke's breath hitched, and a slow smirk curved his lips. "Two years?" he asked, stepping closer.

Anise lifted her chin, her gaze never leaving his. "Two years," she confirmed. "And if I come inside, I can't promise I'll keep that streak going."

Duke's fingers flexed at his sides. He could play it cool, pretend her words didn't ignite something primal inside him—but that wasn't who he was. Instead, he reached for her, trailing a single finger along the bare skin of her arm.

"Then don't," he murmured.

A shaky breath escaped her lips, and then she moved, stepping inside and closing the door behind her. The soft click echoed in the quiet of the room. Duke backed up slowly, leading her deeper inside. The air between them thickened with anticipation, the city lights casting shadows across the sleek, modern space.

She reached for his towel, but he caught her wrist, his grip gentle but firm. "Are you sure?" His voice was rough, strained.

Anise looked up at him, her eyes dark with want. "I wouldn't be here if I wasn't."

That was all he needed. He closed the distance between them, his mouth claiming hers in a kiss that sent a shudder through them. She melted into him, her hands sliding up his damp skin, nails digging slightly as if testing the reality of him.

He lifted her effortlessly, walking them toward his bedroom, where the city lights spilled through the massive windows. He laid her down on his bed, taking his time, savoring every moment, every sigh, every arch of her body. It had been two years for her. He was going to make sure tonight was worth the wait.

Their bodies moved together in a slow, unhurried rhythm, the heat between them building with every touch, every whispered word. He traced the curves of her body with his lips, memorized by the way she responded, the way she gasped his name.

And when they finally came undone, tangled in each other's arms, Duke knew—this wasn't just a moment. This was them, something deeper, something real.

As Anise curled into him, her fingers trailing lazily along his chest, she murmured, "You're trouble, Duke."

He chuckled, pressing a kiss to her forehead. "Yeah," he admitted. "But so are you."

Chapter Seven

He snapped out of the memory when the door to the lounge opened with a soft click, pulling him out of his thoughts. He turned his head, expecting to see some random resident stopping by for a drink. Instead, Cinnamon stepped in, and behind her were her sisters Cayenne and Sage.

Anise's kids. They had never been formally introduced, except for Cinnamon, because she was married to Jax. Cinnamon looked so much like Anise that he blinked again to make sure it wasn't her.

"Oh, sorry," Cinnamon giggled. "Didn't know you were in here, Duke. Leo said he stocked the bar with his new vegan wine and wants us to try it and give him our opinion."

"DJ Duke!" Sage said excitedly. "Sorry to fangirl over you, I know celebrities don't like to be ambushed in their private spaces, but good golly, it's you!"

Duke smiled. "It's me."

Running myself ragged over your mother, as usual. Of

course, he didn't say that part out loud.

Cayenne came and sat across from him. "A little birdie told me you were dating my mother. Is it true?"

"Ooh," Sage sat across from him, "don't lie to us, Cayenne's little birdies are always accurate. The hairdresser's chair is like a confessional."

"I can't confirm nor deny," Duke said lazily.

"We are all adults here, Duke," Cayenne said. "Spill the beans. Are you the one that has Mom so happy these days?"

"Leave the man alone," Cinnamon called from the bar. "Would you like to taste the wine, Duke?"

"No thanks," Duke said. "I'm having the Cinnamon Jade."

"That's my favorite too," Cinnamon said smugly.

"Do you know I'm the only one who doesn't have a wine named after herself?" Cayenne said bitterly. "There's Rosemary Ruby, same as my grandmother; Anise Crystal, same as my mother; Cinnamon Jade, same as Miss Smug over there; and Sage Amethyst, after the little sister; and Valerian Jett, my baby nephew. Even my baby nephew has a wine named after him."

Duke chuckled. "It's a cool way to be immortalized."

"My namesake wine was a limited edition," Sage said happily. "You know, a cooler way to be immortalized is to have a flower named after you. My husband is working on a hibiscus with my name. He's calling it the Sage Whitlock."

Duke smiled. Sage had been married for a few months now and was obviously still in the giddy honeymoon stage. Every statement going forward was going to be 'my husband this, my husband that.' Bruce Whitlock was a lucky man. Anise was quite proud of her girls and their relationships.

Cinnamon joined them with drinks in hand. Her sisters all took a glass.

"I like the color, deep red, almost black," Cayenne said,

taking a sip. "It's not bad. I'm no connoisseur, but it tastes okay to me."

"It's good," Sage said. "What makes a wine vegan, anyway?"

"The process," Duke said. "Leo would be better at explaining, but it has to do with how they filter the wine. Traditional winemaking sometimes uses animal-derived products like egg whites or fish bladder to clarify the wine. Vegan wine uses plant-based or mineral alternatives."

Cinnamon nodded. "That's right. Leo was going on and on about it the other day. No animal byproducts, just pure fermented goodness."

Sage made a face. "Fish bladder? That's… unsettling."

Cayenne smirked. "And yet you're still drinking it."

Sage shrugged. "I'm already committed, and this one isn't made from fish bladder. Weren't you listening? It's vegan."

Duke chuckled, swirling his own drink as the sisters debated the merits of vegan wine. It was strange sitting here with them, Anise's daughters, listening to their easy banter. Seeing them up close, seeing how much of her was reflected in each of them, made it hit differently.

"You never answered the question," Cayenne said, fixing him with a pointed look.

Duke raised a brow. "Which one?"

"Are you the reason our mother's been smiling more lately?"

Cinnamon groaned. "Cayenne, seriously?"

"What? It's a fair question." Cayenne leaned in, her expression mischievous. "Listen, we're not trying to scare you off or anything. We just want to know where things stand."

Sage nodded. "Yeah, we don't get all up in Mom's business, but we can tell when something—or someone—is making a difference in her life."

Duke exhaled, setting his drink down. He wasn't one to spill personal details. Still, something about their curiosity, their protective energy, made him respect them even more.

"I care about your mother," he said simply.

Cayenne arched a brow. "That's vague."

"It's the truth," Duke countered. "She's an incredible woman. Complicated, stubborn, and unpredictable as hell—but incredible."

Sage grinned. "Sounds like Mom, alright."

Cinnamon sighed, sipping her wine. "Well, just so you know, we're not the overprotective type. Mom can handle herself. And for the record, we have never been introduced to anyone she dates. She is notoriously private about her personal life, and we tend to respect those boundaries."

"Why do you think she's so guarded with her relationships?" Duke asked Cinnamon.

"Apart from the media furor when she breaks up with them?" Cinnamon raised an eyebrow. "Well, there's the issue of her feeling like a failure when something ends. She has, to my knowledge, never had a truly long-term relationship. She gets bored easily."

Duke processed her words, trying to understand. "So, she's afraid of getting hurt again?"

Cinnamon nodded slowly. "Exactly. And maybe part of her doesn't think she deserves something lasting. But that's just me speculating, you know. She's never actually opened up about it, at least not to me. Her therapist, I'm sure, gets an earful."

"How would you feel if she had another child?" Duke asked.

"Good God, is she pregnant?" Cayenne whispered.

"No," Duke frowned, "just asking random questions."

Sage chuckled. "I wouldn't mind. Mom once said she wished she had a chance to do parenting right. I hear mothers in their forties do a better job than in their twenties."

"Not necessarily," Cinnamon said, "but I hear the reasoning."

"It would take some getting used to if Mom had a baby," Cayenne shrugged, "but it would be interesting. My daughter is five months old; her aunt or uncle would be younger."

"Lots of families have that dynamic," Cinnamon said. "Younger aunts and uncles. Fair warning, Anise was not a traditional mother to us. She had me when she was thirteen, a child herself, and then Cayenne and Sage in her late teens. By the time she was in her mid-twenties, she was a divorcee. She left us a lot with our nannies while growing up. It would be interesting to see her as a mature mother doing the everyday routine."

Duke listened carefully, his mind processing everything Cinnamon was sharing. He had always known Anise had a complicated relationship with her past, but hearing it from her daughters gave him a deeper understanding.

"Sounds like she had to grow up really fast," he said, his voice thoughtful. "I can see how that would affect how she approaches relationships and motherhood."

Cinnamon nodded, her gaze distant. "Yeah, she never had the luxury of being a carefree teenager or young adult. Everything came fast—having kids and being a mom before she really had the chance to figure herself out. She didn't have the normal experiences that most people do, and I don't think she wants to give up her freedom to return to a point in her life where she felt less free, if you know what I mean."

"I know what you mean," Duke nodded.

"She'd have to love a man deeply and without reserve to introduce him to us or to have his baby," Cayenne said, taking a sip of her wine.

"He'd be a rare one," Sage agreed.

Cinnamon looked at him with sympathy. "And it would take a rare man who loved her just as deeply to understand and respect her decision and let her make up her mind without pressuring her."

Duke nodded, the weight of their words settling in.

"I get it," he said quietly.

He had a lot of thinking to do. Maybe he wouldn't send Anise a goodbye text just yet. He could exercise a bit more patience with her; after all, he had been patient for nearly three years—what's another three months? But he wouldn't be strung along while she figured out whether she loved him or wanted to marry him. To borrow from Chex's cat metaphor, she was no longer a feral cat; she was at least partially tamed, and he was willing to wait until she was ready to trust him completely. But he wasn't going to be her emotional safety net forever. She would have to take the leap if she truly wanted something with him.

Cayenne, ever perceptive, raised her glass, breaking his internal deliberation. "It's not always easy, being with someone who's as complicated as our mom. She doesn't do things halfway."

Duke nodded. "True."

Cinnamon smiled at him as if reading his mind. "I'm glad we had this chat, Duke. Now, onto other topics—tell us about your next song."

"I was thinking of doing a cover of Luther Vandross' 'Secret Love,'" Duke said. "My studio applied for the rights to cover it, and it came through."

"Oh boy," Sage giggled. "I wonder what inspired that."

"Take a wild guess," Duke said, a sly grin forming on his face. "In fact, I just might join my producer at the studio to record it earlier than I had planned."

Chapter Eight

"He left for Ridgeview today," Anise said to Jada as soon as she opened the door. "He didn't even give me a chance to tell him what I think about surrogacy or any of it. He left here last night in a huff and then left me a stinking little note a few hours ago telling me to 'do me' and he would 'do him.' What does that even mean?"

"So that's the emergency?" Jada raised her eyebrows. "You said it was life and death. I didn't even change into street clothes."

"And to think I was going to remove my birth control chip for him, the dweeb," Anise sputtered.

Jada grimaced. "Can I come in?"

"Yep," Anise nodded, opening the door wider. "I was a fool. I was going to upend my life for Duke Oneil Jones, and he didn't even stick around to see me make a fool of myself. He wants a child so badly that he was going the surrogate route, and I thought to myself, 'Would it be so bad if I had another kid or two?' I love babies. I never had a problem getting pregnant in the past."

"You love babies," Jada repeated, sitting on the couch.

"And I love Duke," Anise said. "I mean, I love him deeply. Of course, I've never told him. I don't want him to get too complacent with me."

"No chance of that happening," Jada murmured. "There is no complacency with you, ever."

"Are you shading me or agreeing with me?" Anise looked at Jada sharply.

Jada opened her mouth to answer, but Anise started talking again. "Maybe I shouldn't be a mother. I forgot Cinnamon in the car once, and I drove away and left Cayenne when we were at the supermarket. And the nannies had to remind me about important dates for my children. I couldn't remember when they were supposed to get their relevant shots, play dates, or school trips."

"You weren't a poor mother, just a woman with hyperactivity disorder. You made it work, though," Jada said helpfully. "You always said you got them the best nannies money could buy."

"Yes, I made it work, but they were girls. They are easier," Anise sat down abruptly. "Suppose I have sons? I don't know a thing about raising a boy. And what about the name? Do you know how many months it took me to come up with the name Valerian Jett for my grandson? What would I call a boy?"

"Fennel Jasper, Clove Sterling, Coriander Slate," Jada said helpfully. "Or better yet, don't name him a spice and a stone. What about just a stone? There are some really cool stone names. Did you take your meds this morning?"

"Nope," Anise said. "I was so distraught when I got the message from Duke. I think he wants to derail me."

Jada sighed and leaned back against the couch. "Duke isn't trying to derail you. He's just giving you space."

"I specifically told him I would sleep on it, and he just left me a note instead of waiting to hear what I had to say. And what does he mean by 'you do you'?" She threw up her hands. "What am I supposed to do with that? Just sit here and stew about the meaning of things while he goes off to Ridgeview? Was he breaking up with me? Are we broken up?"

"You could go after him and ask him just that," Jada said.

Anise gave her a long, blank stare. Then, she blinked. "Go after him?"

"Yes. Pack a bag, hop in your car, and go."

Anise looked skeptical. "Like in those ridiculous romance movies where the heroine chases after the guy at the airport?"

"Exactly like that," Jada said with a grin.

Anise scowled. "That's not my style."

Jada shrugged. "Maybe not. But neither is letting a man you love walk away without putting up a fight."

Anise folded her arms. "I don't chase men."

"No, you don't," Jada agreed, "but you also don't let them get the last word."

Anise's lips twitched. "That's true."

"So?" Jada prompted.

Anise let out a deep sigh. "I'll give him a couple of days. If he doesn't call me, I'll call him, and depending on the temperature of the call, then I'll go. But then again…"

"No, it's a sound plan," Jada said. "It seems as if you didn't need me after all."

****

Two weeks later, he was still giving her the silent treatment.

Anise went through the motions of her day; this was starting to feel a little too much like the first couple of months when she was uncertain about Duke. She used to avoid him for stretches of time while she tried to regulate her emotions around him.

She went to her store every day, moonlighting as a cashier, trying to take her mind off the sudden coolness between them.

Her store manager, Priscilla, came to her during a lull near closing time on her first week. "You usually don't come in so often. What gives?"

"Nothing," Anise shrugged. "Can't a girl come to her own place of business and work the floor now and again?"

Priscilla nodded. "Sure, a girl can do that, but when you do it, I begin to wonder if you heard something or if you're checking up on me. I've been working for you for seven years now. I would hope you trust me by now."

Anise sighed, rubbing her temples. "Of course, I trust you, Priscilla. This isn't about you or the store."

Priscilla studied her, arms folded. "So, what is it about?"

Anise hesitated. She wasn't the kind of woman who spilled her personal business, but Priscilla had been with her long enough to see the signs when something was wrong.

"I have a friend," Anise exhaled sharply. "He's not talking to me. He used to call me at least five times a day, and now there's radio silence."

Priscilla raised an eyebrow. "And that's why you're hiding out here instead of dealing with it?"

Anise scowled. "I'm not hiding. I'm... giving my friend space, keeping myself occupied. Besides, I am driving more sales our way. So many people are coming into the store because of me."

Priscilla scowled. "They are coming in because of your

buy-one-get-one impromptu sale, which you did not discuss with me. Because of the sale, I'm going to have to move up our orders for some items. You're messing with our agreed-upon plan for the next quarter."

"Sorry," Anise leaned against the counter, feeling uncharacteristically drained. "I do ridiculous things when I'm falling apart."

"Can you please do these ridiculous things elsewhere?" Priscilla said. "You told me to put my foot down if you start acting up. This is me putting my foot down. No more unilateral decisions and impromptu sales and no more giving away our merchandise."

"I didn't give away anything," Anise sputtered.

"You gave away three head wraps from the African print collection. May I remind you that they are pure silk and quite expensive?"

Anise pouted. "I vaguely remember that."

"Why don't you just call your friend?" Priscilla asked.

"No!" Anise said. "It would make me look needy. I don't want to seem needy."

"So, what are you going to do?"

Anise frowned. "What do you mean?"

"It sounds like you're cutting off your nose to spite your face," Priscilla said. "Just call your friend already, put yourself out of your misery. And, by extension, me. You hired me to make this place as profitable as it can be. I don't want you to mess with the bottom line. I like my quarterly bonuses. I just bought a house in an expensive neighborhood and now have real bills to pay."

Anise chuckled, then stopped mid-laugh when the shop bell sounded, and her mother walked through the door. "Oh good, my awful week just got worse."

"Could you two not have a quarrel until closing time?"

Priscilla begged. "The last time you two got into it, I couldn't get the staff to leave. They were talking about it for weeks."

"Who did they say won?" Anise asked.

"It was about fifty-fifty," Priscilla said. "Your mother knows a lot of big words; some of them were impressed with that. She called you an emotionally damaged wreck with delusions of grandeur," Priscilla continued. "But you held your own. You called her a bitter narcissist with control issues."

Anise smirked. "Sounds like I won."

Her mother scoffed behind them. "Hardly. You were red in the face by the end, and I didn't even raise my voice."

"Mother," Anise growled.

Priscilla sighed. "You two be nice. It's lovely to see you, Rosemary, our valued customer," she said politely before throwing Anise a warning look.

"I didn't know you'd be here," Anise said.

"Likewise," Rosemary said cheerfully. "Nevertheless, it's always a pleasure to see you. I ran out of my favorite perfume, and your shop is the only one that carries it. Otherwise, I would have to buy it online."

Anise smiled. "And how are you doing, Rosemary?"

"Quite fine," Rosemary said pleasantly. "I don't need to ask how you are. You look a little rough around the edges."

Anise gasped and spun around, looking in one of the mirrors on the counter. "I don't look bad. Why does every word out of your mouth have to be a criticism?"

Rosemary sighed, tilting her head. "It's not a criticism, darling, it's an observation."

Anise narrowed her eyes. "You always say that, like it makes a difference."

Rosemary smiled, completely unbothered. "Well, if the truth stings, maybe it's worth considering."

Anise folded her arms. "I look fine."

Rosemary hummed. "If you say so. But I can tell when my daughter is off her game." She leaned on the counter. "What's wrong?"

Anise hesitated. The last thing she wanted was to give her mother ammunition, but she also knew Rosemary would poke and prod until she got an answer.

"Nothing," she said finally.

Rosemary's lips twitched. "It's a man, isn't it?"

Anise scoffed. "Why do you assume it's a man?"

"Because nothing else gets you this frazzled."

Priscilla, who had been pretending not to eavesdrop, let out a snort from across the store. Anise shot her a glare before turning back to her mother.

"It's nothing," she repeated.

Rosemary's eyes gleamed with amusement. "So defensive. That means I'm right." She reached into her purse and pulled out her wallet. "Fine, keep your secrets. I'll just buy my perfume and go."

Anise exhaled, relieved. She rang up the purchase, but as she handed the bag to her mother, Rosemary patted her hand.

"Men don't respond well to games, sweetheart," she said lightly. "If you want something, go after it. You're your mother's daughter, after all."

Anise stiffened. "I'm nothing like you."

Rosemary smiled knowingly. "If you say so." Then, with a wink, she walked out, leaving Anise fuming.

Priscilla wandered back over, shaking her head. "That woman is something else."

Anise groaned. "She's exhausting."

Priscilla smirked. "She's also right."

Anise turned to glare at her. "Don't start."

Priscilla held up her hands. "I'm just saying, maybe it's time to stop pretending like you don't care. You do."

Anise scowled, but deep down, she knew they were both right. The question was—what was she going to do about it?

Chapter Nine

Duke had moved into his Ridgeview house, which was nicely decorated and picturesque, but he hadn't spent much time there so far. He spent most of his time at Knightsbridge Farm studio. The studio was situated in its own little peaceful enclave on the Farm. It was on a hill overlooking acres of unrelieved greenery. Chex mainly used it in the summers, when he, his wife, son, and new baby girl could spend time in Crimson Hills near family. He had also built cottages around the property where visiting artists could stay.

It was the perfect place to unleash creativity. Duke had to admit, there was something about the space that made it easy to lose himself in the music. The air was crisp, carrying the faint scent of damp earth and freshly cut grass. The rolling fields stretched out beyond the hill, offering a view that was both serene and endless.

He'd spent the last two weeks practically living there, pouring his frustration, confusion, and longing into his work. He barely slept and only ate what Chex's housekeeper prepared. Luckily, she was a good cook and unobtrusive. The beats, the melodies, and the lyrics were his only company for two weeks until Chex showed up.

Chex leaned against the doorframe, arms crossed. "You good, man?"

Duke didn't look up from the mixing board. "Yeah."

Chex let out a skeptical hum. "You sure? 'Cause you've been going at this like you're trying to outrun something."

Duke's fingers stilled on the console. He exhaled, shaking his head. "I'm not running from anything."

Chex snorted. "Right. What did Anise do now? Destroy your furniture, knock your favorite figurine off the shelf?"

Chex was still using cat metaphors for Anise. He went along with it.

"She doesn't want to have my kittens."

Chex nodded. "I thought that was what a surrogate was for?"

"Yep, but I'm not totally sold on it," Duke shrugged. "Not unless she is. I asked her about it, and she said she would sleep on it, but like a coward, I didn't want to hear her response. Haven't spoken to her in two weeks."

"Mmm," Chex said, settling into the chair across from Duke. "So let me get this straight—you asked her to make a life-changing question, then dipped before she could answer?"

Duke exhaled heavily, rubbing a hand over his face. "It sounds bad when you say it like that..."

Chex chuckled. "That's because it is bad. Real bad." He leaned forward, resting his elbows on his knees. "You love her?"

Duke shot him an irritated look. "What kind of question is that?"

"A relevant one."

Duke exhaled. "Yeah, I love her."

"Then what the hell are you doing?"

Duke was quiet for a moment, staring at the blinking lights on the console. "I don't know," he admitted. "I just—if she says no, then what? That means she doesn't see a future with me. That means I'm wasting my time."

Chex shook his head. "No, that means she's making a decision for herself. Which is fair, considering you asked her to sign up for something major. But you ghosting her over it? That's weak, man."

Duke scowled. "I didn't ghost her. I—" He sighed, realizing how stupid his argument sounded. "I needed space."

"Nah," Chex said. "You needed control. And when you thought you might not get what you wanted, you ran."

Duke frowned, but he didn't argue. Maybe Chex was right. Maybe he was running.

Chex stood, stretching. "You can keep hiding out here, acting like a tortured artist, or you can man up and talk to her. But if you keep dragging this out, don't be surprised if she makes the decision for you."

Duke's stomach twisted at the thought. After two weeks of silence and distance, what if she already had?

****

"Just saying hi," he texted Anise before he drove out of Knightsbridge Farm. He didn't expect a response. She was probably mad at him.

He was pleasantly surprised when she wrote back, hi.

"Are you okay?" he asked, searching for something to say.

"Fine. Peachy. On top of the world. My boyfriend told me to do me, and he'd do him, and then ghosted me for two weeks. How else would I feel?"

Duke actually chuckled. He could imagine her punching out every letter angrily. "I was in the studio, trying to blow off some steam."

"So are you less steamy now?" Anise asked.

"I feel tired," he responded. "My sister and Alyssa are due to come by today. They are spending some time at the house, so I am going to the house to meet them. I am driving out now. Talk to you at another time."

"Whatever," was the response.

Duke smiled. She was well and truly mad at him.

Good. That meant she still cared.

He thought about calling her to hear her voice, just to test the waters. But he knew better. Anise would hang up on him. This wasn't their first song and dance; they had been here several times before, especially in the early days. He thought about their last major blow nearly a year ago.

He had been smarting from the fact that they went to a function where her mother was the MC, and she had almost spazzed out at the idea of him meeting her mother as anything other than a friend.

"We're two and a half years in. What's the harm in being introduced as your boyfriend?"

"You don't know my mother," Anise had hissed. "If we were going public, she is the last one I want to find out."

"I thought you said you and your mom were in a better place now that you went to counseling together?" he had asked, confused.

"The counseling didn't work," Anise said through gritted teeth. "She is still the same old judgmental, insufferable narcissist who thinks she knows everything about me but never actually listens."

Duke had been taken aback. He knew Rosemary had

been tough on Anise growing up, but he thought things had improved.

"She still second-guesses everything I say and has to give her two cents about things happening in my life like she is some authority," Anise continued, her voice thick with frustration. "And she still thinks I am literally mentally impaired. She knows nothing about ADHD and refuses to be informed about it. I can't deal with her—" She cut herself off and shook her head. "Forget it."

Duke had reached for her hand, but she pulled away. "Anise—"

"No. I don't want to talk about this with you. Rosemary is my mother, but not family."

"Then what about your kids?" Duke had asked. "Why can't I meet them as someone important to you?"

"Because I don't introduce anyone to them!" Anise had said. "You were so easygoing when we first dated. Why are you demanding more from me?"

"That's usually how people are," Duke said. "When you care about someone, you grow to expect more."

"I don't know if this is working for me anymore," Anise huffed.

And that had been the end of the conversation. She shut down, and he shut up. He wasn't sure why he let it go, but maybe he didn't want to push her. They had stopped talking, and four weeks later, she had shown up at his door.

"I am sorry," she had said, her eyes filled with remorse. "I miss you."

"I miss you too," he had opened the door wider and watched as she walked in.

"This is for you," she handed him a box with her apartment's access key. "That's my copy. It's a big step for me."

He had looked at it solemnly. "Okay, maybe I should give you mine too."

He went in search of his copy and handed it to her.

"So what does this mean?" he asked as they stared at each other.

"It means trust and commitment," Anise inhaled shakily. "I've never given a man the keys to my place before."

"I guess this is a step in the right direction," he murmured, pulling her closer.

"It also means that if we are going to truly break up, then we hand back each other the keys."

"Okay," Duke whispered in her hair.

"It will take the guesswork out of our disagreements."

Duke chuckled. "Are you anticipating more disagreements?"

"Of course," Anise sighed.

"But at least this way, we'll know when it's really over," she added, her voice quieter, more uncertain.

Duke didn't like the way that sounded. Like she was already bracing herself for the end. Like she still didn't trust that he wasn't going anywhere.

He pressed a kiss to her forehead. "Or maybe it just means we'll keep finding our way back to each other."

Anise exhaled a shaky breath but didn't respond.

Now, sitting in his car, Duke tapped his fingers on the steering wheel, thinking back on that moment. It had felt like progress. Like she was finally letting him in, even if it was on her own terms. But here they were again, back in the same old cycle.

Maybe that's just how they worked—two people too stubborn for their own good, circling each other, pushing and pulling, never fully letting go.

His phone buzzed. It was Anise. Forget it. I don't even

know why I texted.

Duke smirked. That was textbook Anise—act like she didn't care, then double back just to make sure he knew she did.

He texted back. Maybe you miss me desperately and are happy we are talking again.

There was a long pause before she finally replied.

Don't flatter yourself.

Duke chuckled. Yeah, she still cared. And that was enough for now.

Chapter Ten

"**O**h my goodness," Deanna kept gushing through every room she went through. "I love this place. It's nicer than Jairo's. Kendrea really outdid herself on yours."

"It's not nicer than Jairo's," Duke said. "She just did it to fit my taste. I told her to make the décor musical."

"And she did just that," Deanna whistled. "The attention to detail, the color scheme, the little nods to all your songs. It's perfect."

Duke rubbed his chin. "Yeah, she really nailed it. I gave her a few ideas, but she took them to a whole other level."

Deanna wandered into the living room and ran a hand over the deep velvet of the couch. "You need to throw a housewarming party. I want to see people's reactions when they step in here. It's a masterpiece."

Duke chuckled. "I'm not sure about a party. I like to keep my private life private."

"I know," Deanna snorted. "I still don't know who your

secret girlfriend is."

"Not my choice," Duke said. "The woman in question is even more private than I am."

Deanna grunted. "When can I see the guest house?"

"Now," Duke said. "I'll show you around and give you the keys."

"I may never leave here," Alyssa said, coming downstairs. "I chose one of the guest rooms. It was hard choosing since all of them are nice."

"I am hardly here," Duke said. "There is a housekeeping service that comes in twice per week. I may have to get someone on a more permanent basis, though, because of the cooking. I would poach Chex's housekeeper if I could, but Chex would not have it."

"Until I get around to hiring someone, you'll have to find your own food in the meantime."

"Are you kidding? That's no problem. Cooking here would be a dream," Alyssa whispered. "The whole setup is a dream come true. Thank you so much for letting me stay here, Duke."

"No problem," Duke shrugged. "Just don't disturb me with conversation when I'm trying to write."

"You won't even know I'm here," Alyssa grinned. "I'll be the quietest houseguest you've ever had. My schedule is kind of packed too. I go to work in the mornings and have class until six. I'll only be free on the weekends."

"Come on," Deanna said. "Come show me the guest house."

Duke nodded. "Let's walk this way."

He led Deanna through the mudroom at the back and along a pathway that led to a guest cottage. It was tucked beneath the shade of towering palms, with warm ambient lighting casting a cozy glow over the porch. The cottage was a whole mood—light and airy, it felt like beach house chic with its soft white walls, rattan furniture, and sheer curtains billowing slightly in the evening breeze. Hints of blue and sandy beige accented the space, giving it a relaxed, coastal feel. A woven jute rug lay beneath a low wooden coffee table, and the sectional was covered in plush linen cushions that practically begged to be lounged on.

Deanna stepped inside, eyes wide with appreciation. "Oh wow. This is different from the main house but in the best way. It's like stepping into a vacation."

Duke leaned against the doorframe, arms crossed. "Figured I'd switch it up. The main house is all about the music—this place is for unplugging."

"This is stunning. The finishes, the textures... I love the shiplap ceiling." Deanna said. She stepped inside and spun in a slow circle, taking it all in. "This is nicer than most people's actual homes." She pointed toward the open-concept kitchen. "Look at the finishes—marble countertops, top-of-the-line appliances—wait, is that a built-in espresso machine?"

Duke nodded. "Yeah, Kendrea insisted on that. Said my guests should be spoiled."

"Okay, now I really don't want to leave." Deanna dropped onto the plush sectional and sank into it with a sigh. "Tell me again why you're not renting this out to celebrities?"

Duke scoffed. "Because I don't need the money, and I'd rather know who's staying here."

"Right, right." Deanna stretched, looking up at the high wood-beamed ceiling. "I'm telling you, Duke, you're sitting on a goldmine. This place is a luxury stay."

Duke nodded. "I'm happy you like it. I'll leave you to it."

"No, wait," Deanna whispered. "I want to ask you something."

"What?" Duke asked impatiently.

"It's none of my business."

Duke chuckled. "Okay, this should be interesting. A sentence starting off with 'It's none of my business' usually is."

"I just want to know why you are considering hiring a surrogate to have a baby."

"Alyssa blabbed, didn't she?"

"Yep," Deanna nodded. "She said she found the brochures."

"The lady at the clinic gave me a bunch," Duke nodded.

"So what gives?" Deanna asked. "Is your girlfriend unable to have your baby?"

"I don't think so. But she doesn't want to have any more children—she already has three adult children."

"Ooh, an older woman," Deanna whistled.

"She is just seven years older," Duke shrugged.

"Who is this older woman?" Deanna looked intrigued. "What's wrong with her? Why haven't you introduced her to us if you are serious about her? You had us meet Madge days after you met her."

"Nothing is wrong with my current girlfriend. She's super private," Duke shrugged. "I've never been officially introduced to her family either."

"Is she a criminal like Madge?" Deanna raised an eyebrow.

"No," Duke said, "far from it, she wouldn't kill anyone. Well, except for her ex, he kind of deserved it. He molested little children."

"You are dating Anise Crystal?" Deanna whispered, shocked. "The Anise Crystal?"

"Is Anise Crystal the only woman in Jamaica who almost killed her ex-husband when she found him molesting his kids?"

"Yes!" Deanna nodded. "Well, obviously not, but she's the

most famous one. I watched that interview she did on Claire Talk with mom, and it made the two of us so emotional. We would have liked nothing more than to meet her and give her a hug. She's a brave woman."

"And smart and funny," Duke added. "But we are having some issues right now."

Deanna nodded. "You want children, and she doesn't."

Duke let out a slow breath, running a hand over his head. "Yeah. She has her children already. She wasn't planning on having any at this stage of her life."

Deanna sat up, her expression thoughtful. "But you want to be a father."

"I do," Duke admitted. "I've always wanted kids. And I thought… maybe she'd be open to it if I found another way. But the last time we talked about surrogacy, we had a fight."

Deanna frowned. "What kind of fight?"

Duke exhaled sharply, pushing off the doorframe and pacing a little. "She thinks I'm trying to trap her into a deeper commitment, that if we have a kid—biological or not—it'll tie us together in a way she's not sure she wants."

Deanna winced. "Oof. That's… tough."

"Yeah." He scrubbed a hand over his face. "I get it, kind of. She spent years fighting to protect her kids and rebuild her life. One of her daughters put it succinctly—she never had a chance to be a child herself. I don't think Anise wants to be doing diapers and midnight feedings at this stage of her life."

"But you do."

Duke looked at her, jaw tight. "Yeah, I do."

Deanna sighed. "So what's the solution? Are you willing to give up fatherhood for her?"

Duke hesitated. That was the real question, wasn't it?

"I don't know," he admitted. "I love her, but this… it's

not a small thing. I keep thinking maybe she'll change her mind, but I also don't want to pressure her into something she doesn't want."

Deanna folded her arms. "You have to be real with yourself, Duke. If this is a deal-breaker for you, dragging it out won't help either of you."

"I know," Duke said, his voice rough. "I just don't know if I can walk away."

Deanna stepped forward, her gaze steady. "Then you need to talk to her. For real, this time. No, hoping she'll come around, no avoiding the hard conversation. If she's not open to it, you need to decide if that's something you can live with."

Duke let out a slow breath. "Yeah. You're right."

"Of course I am," Deanna smirked. "Now, let's talk about something less depressing. Like how Michael and I may never want to find another place to live after seeing this guesthouse."

Duke chuckled, but the weight of the conversation still sat heavily on his chest. He had some serious thinking to do. And sooner rather than later.

****

Alyssa was reeling from the conversation she had just overheard. She had eagerly followed Duke and Deanna to the guesthouse, only to hear that he was in a relationship with Anise Crystal. The notorious Anise Crystal. The feisty, fierce, no-nonsense woman who had overcome all sorts of hellish obstacles in her life to become a thriving, successful businesswoman. Richard Greystone's love child. One of the richest women in Jamaica.

Alyssa hurriedly went back to the house before Duke

could see her. She had admittedly had a loose interest in Anise for a few years now, ever since hearing her story about her childhood abuse on Claire Talk.

She had to admit she had been one of the scores of people who, upon hearing that Richard Greystone had left an equal portion of his fortune to Anise, assumed they had been having an affair and that Anise had coerced him into leaving some of his wealth to her. To her shame, she had gone with the more sensational narrative when she had just heard the news.

This made her question—what part of Anise Crystal's life was real, and what part was just media fodder? She certainly couldn't be the rabid femme fatale who changed rich boyfriends every other month like they portrayed.

Duke said they had been together for three years and that he loved her—which wasn't saying much; he had loved Madge. His woman-picker was broken. Or was it? She didn't know Anise Crystal. Apart from her sporadic interviews on Claire Talk, what did she know about the woman?

She went out on the patio and laid down, scrolling through the Claire Talk videos on YouTube with Anise in them. She was watching the one on celibacy when Duke came in.

"How about takeout?" he asked behind her. "What would you like?"

Alyssa jumped and looked at him guiltily.

"Er… food," she muttered.

He smiled. "I won't ask what you were watching. You seem guilty. Whatever it is, I'm not judgmental."

"I, er, overheard you and Deanna," Alyssa said. "I came to check out the guesthouse. I didn't mean to eavesdrop."

"That's okay," Duke shrugged.

"So, I came back here looking for some Anise Crystal interviews to see what she was like."

"Cool," he said. When he heard Anise's voice, he came closer.

"I don't sleep around casually," Anise said. "I heard that a side effect of being molested at a young age is promiscuity. I was the anomaly. I wouldn't let just anyone touch me. I had to feel safe, respected, and in control of my body. Sex was never a coping mechanism for me—it was something sacred, something I had to be sure about."

Duke let out a slow breath as he listened. Alyssa watched his face carefully, noting the way his jaw tightened slightly, the flicker of something in his eyes—pride, admiration, maybe even love.

"You knew that about her?" Alyssa asked, keeping her tone light, even as curiosity burned inside her.

He nodded. "Of course. We talk about everything. She never tried to be what people expected her to be." His voice softened. "She's one of the strongest people I know."

Alyssa studied him. "You really love her, don't you?"

Duke didn't answer right away. Instead, he reached for his phone and placed an order for their food. When he finally met her gaze, his expression was unreadable.

"I do." The words were simple but firm. "It's not always easy. She's not easy. But she's real."

Alyssa exhaled, feeling something settle in her chest. Anise Crystal wasn't just some tabloid fantasy, some scandalous, untouchable figure. She was a woman who had lived, survived, and thrived on her own terms. And Duke—broken picker or not—had chosen her.

"So," Alyssa said, "she doesn't want any more kids, huh?"

"She never outrightly said that," Duke said. "She did say she would think about it. I came here before she could answer one way or another. One of her daughters did say it would take a special man for her to have kids with and introduce to her family. I've been chewing over that. I guess I'm not special to Anise. But I keep hanging on, hoping for change. I thought she and I were together long enough to be tried and true."

Alyssa shook her head. "In order to be tried and true, you have to be tested."

Duke let out a dry chuckle, rubbing a hand over his face. "And you don't think three years is a test?"

Alyssa shrugged. "Three years can be comfortable. A real test? That's when things get uncomfortable. That's when you ask for more than the other person is willing to give and see what they do, like the surrogacy idea, or you create a situation where they have to choose you or leave."

Duke sighed, sinking into the chair across from her. "With the surrogacy thing, she never said no."

"She never said yes either," Alyssa pointed out gently.

Silence stretched between them. The only sound was the occasional murmur from the video still playing on Alyssa's phone. Anise's voice was steady and sure.

"I believe in love," Anise was saying. "But I don't believe in losing myself for it. I won't shrink to fit someone's expectations. Either they love me as I am or don't love me at all."

Duke inhaled sharply, and Alyssa knew the words hit home.

"So, what's a deal breaker for you in a relationship, Anise?" Claire asked.

Anise paused. "Well, I have dozens of deal breakers. Hello, have you seen the state of my relationships? They go south quickly."

"But what's the one," Claire insisted, "that will make you say, 'Hell no, I am outta here, stat'?"

"Cheating," Anise said. "If he cheats, that's it. I'm not the forgiving type, nor the trusting type. I figure, though, that when I finally find a man I love totally and completely, I may change my stance on all of these deal-breakers. I may become that woman who will give a man a second chance. I don't know! Who knows?"

Alyssa smiled slyly. "You want to know if she loves you like you love her?"

"No," Duke shook his head. "Whatever you're thinking, don't think it."

"Come on, Duke," she said. "She said it herself, you need to test her."

"No thanks." Duke stood up.

"Don't worry," Alyssa said. "I'm on it."

Duke glared at her. "Alyssa, please…"

"I kind of feel obligated to help you out," Alyssa said. "You're my friend. I didn't scream hard enough about Madge, and you married her and were so brokenhearted. I felt it for you. I don't want this to be round two with your heart. I'm going to force Anise's hand. When I'm done, she'll either fight for you or let you go. One way or another, you'll have your answer."

Duke groaned, rubbing his hands over his face. "Alyssa, this is a terrible idea."

"No, it's an honest idea." Alyssa's eyes gleamed with mischief, but there was something serious beneath it. "She's a tough woman, Duke. If she really loves you, she'll fight for you. And if she doesn't…" She shrugged. "Better to know now than waste more time hoping."

Duke exhaled, shaking his head. "I don't like this."

"You're not supposed to," Alyssa said sweetly. "Just sit back and let me work. Besides, I am going to test you too."

He pointed a finger at her. "Don't take it too far."

She smirked. "Me? Never. I may need outside help, but I

won't give you any details."

Duke groaned again. He had a bad feeling about this.

Alyssa, however, was already mentally crafting a plan. If Anise Crystal loved Duke, she'd either stand her ground and fight for him or walk away. And Alyssa was determined to find out which.

Chapter Eleven

Anise felt like a woman in withdrawal. She hadn't spoken to Duke in one month. They texted, but it was usually along the lines of "Heading into the studio, are you okay?" followed by a terse "Fine" from her. She wanted to see and speak to him so badly. This wasn't like the early days when she could just show up at his apartment. He was all the way in Montego Bay, and she had no reason to go there and just show up.

She called Jada to come up with a reason.

Jada was at a bridal expo, and the background was noisy.

"Why don't you come down here?" Jada offered. "I got a booth at the last minute."

Anise grudgingly agreed. At the last bridal show she attended, a reporter wrote a long article speculating about her getting married. And because it was juicy gossip, they listed the long line of men she had supposedly dated and was currently dating, but some men on the list she had never even heard of. It had given her a thrill to know that Duke hadn't been on the list, and they were a year in.

For some strange reason, the media loved her. She was portrayed as a sassy, independent woman who didn't take nonsense from anyone. It was flattering but also exhausting. The truth was, she didn't feel nearly as confident as they made her out to be. Especially not now, when she was practically itching to hear Duke's voice.

She sighed and grabbed her keys. Maybe a bridal expo would be a distraction. Maybe she'd find some ridiculous reason to head to Montego Bay after.

When she arrived at the expo, Jada was in full business mode, directing a couple toward a display of gorgeous custom wedding dresses. "Give me five minutes," Jada mouthed before turning back to her clients with a bright smile.

Anise wandered through the crowd, keeping her sunglasses on even indoors. She was not in the mood to be recognized. The last thing she needed was another speculation piece about whether she was secretly engaged.

Her fingers itched to check her phone to see if Duke had messaged her. But no. If she gave in and texted him first, she'd feel weak.

Then her phone buzzed.

Her heart skipped. It was Duke. He texted, "You okay?"

She smiled and texted back, "Good, and you?"

Duke texted back, "In the studio all day, just checking in with my favorite girl."

Her smile couldn't get wider.

"I needed models," Jada said behind her. "But I wasn't planning to display in Kingston this year. I wanted to save up everything for Montego Bay. Bridal Magazine is giving the best bridal display designer a cover on their magazine and a whole article about them on the inside. I want that, I really, really want that, but now I feel basic. Look at Tarique Chang; he has models. He went all out."

Anise spun around and looked over at Tarique's booth. "Yep, all ages and sizes. Aren't those just his family members? Isn't that his grandmother, Lorna?"

"It is Lorna," Jada nodded. "She is getting married again. It was all over the news."

"I hope it's not to a guy half her age who's after her money."

"She has more than money going for her. She's still pretty," Jada snorted. "You wish you could pull a man at eighty like her."

"No, you wish," Anise chuckled. "You're here envying Tarique's granny; you're just twenty-seven years old."

Jada laughed. "I can pull men, just not while I'm still married to Richard Tinsdale. I have this old-fashioned notion that you're off the market once you're married."

"Then get a divorce," Anise shrugged.

"About that," Jada murmured. "I'm going to take up Richard's offer to try again."

"You are?" Anise widened her eyes.

"Yep," Jada nodded. "I told him when I do the wedding expo in Montego Bay, I'll stay at his place at Ridgeview, not our old house—too many bad memories."

Anise nodded. "When is the expo in Montego Bay?"

"In three weeks," Jada said. "I am planning to go all out there, decorate my booth, display my dresses to the best advantage, but Tarique here is showing that I'm going to need models. Hopefully, it will enhance my display and nudge Bridal Magazine in my direction."

Anise nodded. "So you're going full wedding?"

Jada nodded. "Yes, why not? I'll do other designs, like the mother-of-the-bride dresses and bridesmaids. However, working with your girls these past couple of years has wet my appetite for the bridal market."

"Yep, people pay an arm and a leg for a wedding dress," Anise said. "It makes sense to switch."

"What are you and your girls doing three weeks from now?" Jada asked. "And your mother? Hell, even throw in Grandma Saidie. You're all modelesque. Tarique can't compete with that if I have all the Spices in one place. In fact, I'd ask them to wear their wedding dresses. I designed all of them, and each of them was truly unique. If they agree, I could get that magazine feature—I can just feel it."

She looked at Anise assessingly. "I would have to design one for you. Is there a style you like?"

"I never said I would model for you," Anise frowned. "And you don't know that any of my girls would be available. Three weeks is short notice. As for Grandma Saidie, she doesn't like to leave her house. Do you know how often I've tried to convince that woman to go to a spa and take some time for herself, but she always says no?"

"But Grandma Saidie owes me," Jada said. "She would do anything for me. I went to her church when I lived with my mother in Portmore. I saved her life once."

"Really?" Anise said. "Why didn't you tell me that?"

"It was nothing, really. I didn't even know that's what I did. We had a church potluck, and this church sister carried bammy as her contribution. I accidentally knocked Grandma Saidie's plate out of her hand before she could eat it. It was purely accidental, but we later found out that the cassava in the bammy hadn't been processed properly, and several people were rushed to the hospital with cyanide poisoning. Because I knocked out Grandma Saidie's plate, she said I saved her life. She came and thanked me and said she owes me, and I can collect anytime I want. Now is the time for collection, I really need her now. I want an attractive late-seventies, early-eighties lady to counteract Tarique's grandma."

Anise chuckled. "Okay then, I guess she owes you."

"She told me that I had great things ahead," Jada said proudly.

"That's generic," Anise snorted. "Grandma Saidie likes to think she's a prophetess."

"But didn't you say she has a sixth sense when it comes to choosing spouses?" Jada raised an eyebrow. "Have you introduced her to Duke yet?"

"No," Anise hissed.

"So sad, you didn't give him the Grandma Saidie treatment when you told all your girls that they should take their prospective spouses to her because she can tell when a man is good. Are you afraid of what she'll say about Duke?"

"Oh, shut it," Anise said.

"About the expo," Jada said, "if I can only get you and Grandma Saidie, I'd be fine. I'd hire some ladies from a local agency for the day."

"Why do you want me?" Anise frowned.

"Because you are the Anise Crystal," Jada said. "Stop acting as if you don't know how famous you are. You didn't come into the arena wearing dark glasses for no reason."

"Famous for nothing," Anise muttered. "Most of the men they link me with, I have never dated, and they go along with the lie for PR purposes."

"There is that, and the fact that you were married to Paul Aubry, the famous sculptor who you almost killed when you found out who he was and what he was about. And you're the love child of the late, great Richard Greystone of Greystone Wines, one of the richest men in Jamaica. Just you posing in a wedding dress will have me featured all over the local news. I have to do a wow dress for you."

"I didn't say I'd do it," Anise pointed out.

"But you will," Jada looked at her slyly. "You wanted an excuse to go to Montego Bay. Where I'm staying is right beside Duke. You'd jump through hoops to have a reason to go to that side of the island and be in his vicinity.

"I'll send you the designs I'm considering for you. I can see you in gold and white. What was your first wedding dress like?"

"Didn't wear one," Anise said. "We went straight to the courthouse. Paul was eager to get married so that Cinnamon could come and live with us, but Grandma Saidie said, 'Hell no. I can see right through that man, and something is not right with him.'"

Jada smiled. "Grandma Saidie does it again. She's a seer for sure. I think our little Montego Bay trip will solve several problems at once. You'll get your excuse to see Duke, and Grandma Saidie can vet him."

****

Anise was in high spirits when she entered the Wilde Building. She hadn't needed to ask Jada for help; it had all landed in her lap. And though modeling a wedding dress wasn't the most desirable thing to do, she would do it.

"Hey, Anise," Leo called.

She stopped at the bank of elevators. "Hey, Leo."

"Thank you for getting Duke to perform at the launch party. I know you don't check your emails or answer calls when you don't feel like it, so I wanted to tell you in person. Your official invitation should be in your mailbox by now. Or you don't check that, too?"

Anise grinned. "I'm not that bad. I answer your calls sometimes."

Leo chuckled. "So, how is it going with you and Duke?"

"None of your business," Anise said snarkily.

"That's no way to talk to your nephew, Aunt Anise," Leo smirked. "Besides, I know that the two of you are an item. I could blab to a gossip rag or two."

"Greystones don't leak stories to the papers," Anise said. "Nice try, though, nephew."

Leo laughed. "Fair enough. But seriously, you two good?"

Anise hesitated. She hated that the answer wasn't a confident yes. "We're... fine."

Leo lifted a skeptical brow. "That 'fine' sounds like a lie."

She sighed, pressing the elevator button again, even though it was already lit. "I haven't seen him in a month."

"Ah," Leo nodded knowingly. "That's why he dropped the cover of Luther Vandross's 'Secret Love' this morning. I heard it while heading to work. Love it. I've always preferred the reggae version of any music and Duke's cover was excellent."

Anise groaned. "He's been busy in the studio. That's an interesting cover."

"Your secret love will never be your true love, I can't be no secret, Annie. It's breakin' my heart." Leo sang.

"He said Annie?" Anise froze.

Leo shrugged. "I swore I heard that."

"Liar," Anise said as they got on the elevator together.

Leo grinned. "Maybe, maybe not. But if he sang that, what are you gonna do about it?"

Anise folded her arms. "Nothing. Absolutely nothing."

Leo scoffed. "Yeah, right. You are already plotting your next move."

She had, but she wouldn't admit that to Leo.

The elevator doors opened to her floor, and she stepped out. "Enjoy your day, nephew. Try not to get caught up in gossiping."

"Try not to pretend you don't miss him," Leo said as the doors slid shut.

Anise exhaled, her heart racing. She pulled out her phone, opened her music app, and searched for the song.

DJ Duke – Secret Love (Reggae Cover).

Her finger hovered over the play button. Did she really want to hear it?

Her resolve cracked and she hit play.

That deep, familiar voice filled her ears, rich and smooth like always. But when he reached that line—"I can't be no secret, Annie, it's breakin' my heart"—her breath caught.

Leo wasn't lying.

Duke had sung an abbreviation of her name. She hoped no one realized that it was her. At least he didn't say Anise.

Her stomach flipped, and her chest tightened.

What the hell was she supposed to do now?

She dialed his number furiously, and a woman answered.

"Where's Duke?" Anise asked impatiently.

"He left his phone at home," the lady said. "Who is this?"

"It doesn't matter," Anise said. "I didn't know Duke had someone staying with him at his new place."

The woman laughed. "You sound jealous. Are you his secret love? Is this Annie?"

Anise growled. "I have no time for your questions. Who the hell is this?"

"His friend, Alyssa. Why are you breaking Duke's heart, Annie?"

"What in the hell..." Anise growled. "It's just a song. Artists sing songs that have nothing to do with their personal lives all the time. As for the rest, I have no comment. What does he have me saved as in his phone?"

"Lover," Alyssa said waspishly.

"Then tell him that Lover called, and he must call me back ASAP," Anise huffed.

"He should have put 'Secret Lover,' Alyssa said lightly, "or Annie."

Anise clenched her jaw. This girl was enjoying this way too much.

"Tell him exactly what I said," she snapped, hanging up before Alyssa could make another witty remark.

Her fingers trembled as she gripped the phone. Who the hell was Alyssa? And why was she at his house answering his phone?

She paced the room, her heart pounding. She needed to calm down. She needed answers.

Instead of sitting around and stewing in her emotions, she grabbed her keys.

Montego Bay wasn't that far, and Duke owed her an explanation.

Chapter Twelve

Anise was on her way out of Kingston when she realized she had no idea where Ridgeview was. She had not packed for this impromptu journey and was no longer irrationally angry. Reasoning had begun to set in. She had heard the name Alyssa several times before. Duke said they were childhood friends. Their parents had wanted their children to marry each other; in fact, his sister, Deanna, was married to Alyssa's brother, Michael.

It was a relief to remember that little tidbit before entering the highway. The next exit would have been a few miles away. She did a U-turn and headed back home feeling stupid.

But what if Duke had changed his mind about Alyssa. What if, in his one-month absence, he had developed feelings for Alyssa.

But that wouldn't be the Duke she knew when he was recording an album he was all in. It was all about the music. She doubted he was having some hot and torrid romance at Ridgeview. Alyssa didn't indicate that she was anything other than a friend.

Still, doubt gnawed at her.

Anise parked outside her apartment and rested her forehead against the steering wheel. What the hell am I doing?

She had spent the past month trying to convince herself that she was okay, that the distance didn't bother her, and that Duke would reach out when he was ready. But one phone call with someone else answering his phone had sent her spiraling.

Get it together, Anise.

She turned on the radio. Claire Talk was on.

"We loved the Secret Love cover released by DJ Duke today. It has been nonstop playing in my house," Claire chuckled. "The question is, who is Annie, and why are you breaking our beloved DJ's heart? What's wrong with you, Annie?"

"Duke is a good man—a rare one in the industry, hell, even in Jamaica. He already got his heart broken by Madge the Murderess. He recovered, and now this. Annie, whoever you are, shame on you!"

With a sigh, Anise turned off the radio, climbed out of the car, and headed inside. She needed a plan—something better than impulsively driving to Montego Bay like a mad woman.

Her phone buzzed just as she kicked off her heels. Duke.

She hesitated for only a second before answering. "Took you long enough."

"Alyssa said you called?" His voice was smooth, amused.

Anise scoffed. "I don't appreciate having some random woman answering your phone and acting like she's your fiancée."

Duke chuckled, "Alyssa is staying at my place for a couple

of weeks. I told you that."

"I didn't remember until I was driving out of Kingston on my way to Mobay, and you did mention that she was staying with you. I was so incensed."

"You were jealous of Alyssa? Duke chuckled.

Anise rolled her eyes. "I don't do jealousy."

Duke laughed. "If it makes you feel better, I haven't seen her much since she moved in. She goes to her office and then attends an in-house course her company is offering."

"Yeah, well, tell her not to answer your phone next time. Why does she feel she can take up your phone and converse with people who call you? I dislike her sense of entitlement."

"I'll talk to her," Duke said.

There was silence for a beat, and then Duke's voice dropped, quieter. "Are you mad at me, Anise?"

Her stomach flipped at the way he said her name.

"I—" She stopped. Was she mad? Or was she just frustrated because she missed him?

"You don't have to say it," Duke murmured. "I get it."

Anise exhaled slowly. "Do you?"

"Yeah." A pause. "I miss you too."

Her throat tightened. She sank onto the couch, staring at the ceiling. "Then come home, Duke."

Another pause. Then, "I will."

"When?"

"When the album is done."

Anise closed her eyes. Typical. She should've been prepared for that answer.

"I'll be back for the Bay Rock launch. Maybe I'll see you then."

"You know I'll be there," Anise said. "About your latest single—"

"Did you like it?" Duke asked.

"Did you have to say, Annie? It's just two letters off from Anise. And you know how much I abhor that nickname."

"I couldn't very well say Anise, could I?" Duke laughed. "Besides, I've been hankering to do a cover of that song since we got together."

"That song does not parallel our situation," Anise said. "The woman in the song is obviously cheating with the man and doesn't want anyone else to know. We are not in that situation—we're keeping a low profile for our sanity's sake. In case you didn't realize, you are a popular musician with a rabid following. I am older than you—"

"By six and a half years, which is negligible," Duke said.

"And I am somewhat notorious myself," Anise continued. "I want privacy. That's not too much to ask, is it?"

"No," Duke said, "but we have no reason to hide when it comes to our families. And that's what gets me. We have a superficial connection. You know what I want, Anise— marriage, children, commitment. I want to grow old with you. I want to wake up next to you every morning, not just when our schedules align. I want more than stolen moments and whispered phone calls. I want a life with you, Anise."

His words sent a shiver down her spine.

"Duke…" she started, but he wasn't done.

"I respect your need for privacy, but I won't pretend like this—us—is just casual. Not to the world, and definitely not to you."

Anise swallowed. He'd never been shy about what he wanted, but hearing it said so plainly, with no room for misinterpretation, made her heart race.

"I just need time," she said, barely above a whisper.

Duke exhaled. "Time for what? To convince yourself you don't want the same things?"

"It's not that simple," she murmured.

"It is for me." His voice was calm but firm. "I love you, Anise."

Her breath caught. He'd said it before, but tonight, it felt heavier. More real.

"I won't force you to say it back," Duke continued, "but I need you to know—no matter how long it takes, I'm not going anywhere."

Anise closed her eyes, her grip tightening on the phone.

She wanted to believe that.

She needed to.

She was more damaged than she thought. What was stopping her from saying the words? What was preventing her from fully committing to Duke?

After they wrapped up the call, she dialed her therapist. Mandy Brooks was on speed dial.

"Come in for a session," Mandy said. "I can fit you in half an hour. Let's ventilate the issues."

Anise chuckled. Mandy loved to ventilate the issues.

****

Mandy's office was fifteen minutes away. It was in a complex that had several health-related specialist practicing there. Anise had been going to her for ten years, but for the past three years, their sessions have been more sparse. They had settled on a medication that worked. She had been happy with Duke. When she needed to ventilate an issue, she did it with him. He was sometimes better than Mandy.

She arrived at the complex, parked her car, and took a deep breath before stepping out. The evening air was cool, carrying the faint scent of rain on the pavement. She smoothed the front of her dress, more out of habit than nervousness, and walked toward the entrance.

The reception area was quiet. A soft instrumental melody played in the background, and the air smelled of lavender and vanilla. Anise checked in with the receptionist and then made her way to Mandy's office.

Mandy was waiting for her at the door, her signature warm but assessing expression in place. "Come in," she said, stepping aside.

Anise entered the familiar space. It had earthy tones, plush chairs, and a framed quote on the wall that read Healing is not linear. She took her usual seat, curling her legs under her. Mandy sat across from her, pen poised to write.

"So," Mandy began, "what needs ventilating?"

Anise let out a slow breath. "Duke."

Mandy's brow lifted slightly. "Ah. You've mentioned before that things were getting serious. What happened?"

"He told me he loves me. Again. He also said he wants marriage, kids, and a whole life together. No more in-between moments."

Mandy studied her for a beat. "And how do you feel about that?"

"I don't know," Anise admitted. "I love him, I do. But when he says those things, pressure builds in my chest. I feel I'm being backed into a corner, even though I know he's not forcing me."

Mandy tapped her pen against the notepad. "Is it fear of commitment? Or fear of something else?"

Anise swallowed. "I don't know."

Mandy gave a slight nod. "Let's explore that, then. When you think about being with Duke permanently, what's the first thought that comes to mind?"

Anise hesitated, then said, "He'll wake up one day and regret choosing me."

Mandy's gaze softened. "Ah. And why do you think that?"

Anise chewed on her lip. "Because... I come with baggage loads of baggage, you know, my baggage, child sex abuse, had my abuser's baby, married a pedophile, dated some really shitty men. I have mommy issues and daddy issues and added to that, I have a mental disorder. Why does he even love me, and how will I know this relationship will not be horrible like all the rest. I don't trust my own judgment."

Mandy's expression remained steady, but her voice was softer. "Anise, you've been through hell. I won't pretend otherwise. And I understand why you don't trust your own judgment. But tell me, has Duke ever given you a reason to doubt him?"

Anise opened her mouth, then shut it. She wanted to say yes because it would be easier. Because it would give her an excuse to keep the walls up. But the truth was—no, Duke had never hurt her. Never manipulated her. Never made her feel small or used.

"No," she admitted, voice barely above a whisper.

Mandy nodded. "Then what if, just this once, your judgment is right? What if you actually chose someone good for you?"

Anise blinked rapidly, her throat tightening. "That's the scary part."

Mandy studied her for a long moment. "Because if he's good for you if this is real and healthy, then there's no excuse to run anymore."

Anise let out a shaky breath. "Exactly."

Mandy leaned forward. "Anise, you've survived things most people can't even fathom. You've rebuilt your life, your career, your sense of self. You are strong. But strength doesn't mean shutting love out. It doesn't mean keeping yourself in survival mode when you have a chance to actually live."

Anise stared down at her hands, fingers twisting together. "And what if I let myself believe in this… and I end up wrong again?"

Mandy tilted her head. "What if you let yourself believe in this… and you end up happy?"

The words settled over her, sinking into places she hadn't dared touch.

Could she trust herself? Could she trust him?

Maybe it was time to get out of her own way, close her eyes, and just live.

"You are not unlovable, you are not too old to love and start a family with a man you can finally love." Mindy said, "You are worthy of happiness, Anise. You always have been."

Anise let out a slow breath, her chest tightening with something that wasn't fear for once—but possibility.

Mandy smiled gently. "You don't have to decide everything this evening. But maybe, in the future, you can let yourself believe that love doesn't have to hurt. That this time, it can be different."

Anise nodded, swallowing hard.

Maybe it was time to let herself have this.

Maybe it was time to stop running.

Chapter Thirteen

The courtyard at Greystone Vineyard had been transformed into a breathtaking scene of romance and luxury. Deep red roses cascaded from silver-draped archways, their velvety petals catching the glow of the chandeliers suspended above. Small, round tables covered in shimmering silver tablecloths were set with flickering candles and delicate floral arrangements of crimson lilies and white orchids.

A grand stone fountain sat at the center, its water dyed a soft blush pink, reflecting the warm glow of fairy lights strung between the ivy-covered walls. It was an awe-inspiring sight. Anise and Jada were ushered into the venue and handed a single red rose.

"Ladies, right this way," an usher said deferentially.

"Do you think Duke is here yet?" Anise whispered to Jada.

"Of course," Jada said. "He's probably in his dressing room wondering if you've arrived."

A server stopped and served them wine.

"No alcohol for me," Anise said. "Do you have anything non-alcoholic?"

"Of course," the waiter nodded. "We have a line of mocktails. I will be with you shortly."

"I can't believe you're at a launch for a wine at your own vineyard, and you're not drinking," Jada chuckled.

"I don't like how alcohol makes me feel emotionally unbalanced," Anise said. "I want all my wits about me tonight when I see Duke again. Besides, I know how Bay Rock tastes. I sampled it with and without alcohol during the development process."

"What's that like?" Jada asked. "What does wine taste like without alcohol?"

"It's a little strange at first," she said, taking in the scenery around them. "When you drink it without the alcohol, it's smoother, more subtle. The flavors come through more clearly, and you can really appreciate the layers of fruit and the undertones of bay leaf. It kind of adds a slightly minty, earthy taste to the wine. But when the alcohol's in it, there's that warmth that rounds it all out."

"Sounds like you know your wine," Jada chuckled. "Maybe you're not missing out after all."

Anise laughed lightly, glancing over at the stage where Duke would soon be performing. The anticipation gnawed at her stomach. It had been six weeks since she last saw him. Six whole weeks. Nothing compared to the feeling of being in the same room with him. She could already feel the pull of his presence, even though she hadn't spotted him yet.

As they made their way through the crowd, Anise's eyes flitted over the other guests, but her mind was elsewhere. She was suddenly very aware of how much she had missed Duke—his voice, his touch, the warmth that seemed to radiate from him. She felt a flicker of nervousness that she hadn't expected. Was he still the same? Was she still the same?

Jada leaned in, sensing her friend's quiet tension. "You're overthinking," she murmured. "Relax. Tonight is about you, Duke, and whatever happens. Just let it be."

Anise nodded but wasn't entirely convinced. She could hear the sound of soft laughter and the occasional clink of glasses as the event began to settle into a rhythm.

There were speeches, and dinner was served. Leo did a good job gushing over the latest rollout. And then the MC announced their special guest musician.

"DJ Duke, everybody!"

The crowd cheered as Duke entered the stage.

He was dressed all in black and looked ravishing, even from where she sat.

Jada elbowed her. "Your mouth is open."

Anise chuckled. "He looks so good."

"And sounds even better," Jada said. "I love me some DJ Duke. I hope he does No Promises. I adore that song."

"Here we go," Anise whispered to herself, her heart rate picking up as he stood confidently at the edge of the stage, looking effortlessly cool in a dark shirt open to reveal the column of his neck. He was clean-shaven, muscular, and looked like he could be posing for a magazine. His presence was magnetic, and Anise felt the familiar flutter in her chest at the sight of him.

Her table was close to the stage, and she took him in hungrily.

He caught her eye, and a small, knowing smile tugged at the corner of his lips.

As the crowd quieted, Duke took the microphone. "Good evening, everyone," his voice boomed, rich and smooth, sending a wave of heat through Anise's body. "I'm honored to be here tonight at the Bay Rock launch. This next song is one that's been on my mind for a while. I hope you all enjoy it."

Anise felt a surge of emotion as the first familiar chords of "Secret Love" drifted into the night air.

His voice was even more captivating in person, raw and full of emotion, the song weaving through the atmosphere like a story only the two of them knew. She closed her eyes for a moment, allowing herself to be swept away in the music, the lyrics resonating deep within her.

"I can't be no secret, Annie, it's breakin' my heart..."

She opened her eyes, meeting his gaze again. Duke's expression softened as he continued to sing, and it was clear—this wasn't just a performance for him. The song was personal, and the way he looked at her and sang the words made her heart race.

The song finished, but the emotions lingered. The crowd erupted into applause, but Anise barely heard it, her entire world focused on Duke.

Duke hit song after song, interspersed with some new tracks not yet released.

"Best Valentine's night ever," Jada was rocking and waving, participating with each song except the newer ones. "If only I had a boy valentine. No offense to you, Anise."

Anise chuckled. "None taken."

As the applause died down and Duke made his way off the stage, Anise took a steadying breath. She was about to go to him.

"Alright, enough of the nerves," Jada said with a smirk, giving Anise a playful shove toward the stage. "Go get your man."

Anise chuckled, nodding. "I may leave with him."

"As expected," Jada shrugged. "I am staying till the bitter

end. I want to see if our table will win the gift basket of Greystone Wines. I hope they put an Anise Crystal in it."

"I give you wines all the time," Anise frowned.

"There's nothing like winning it that makes me appreciate it even more," Jada said contemplatively.

Anise chuckled and watched Duke slip backstage. With a deep breath, she followed.

The backstage area was quieter and less chaotic. It smelled faintly of wine, mixed with the scent of Duke's cologne. Before she could even find him, she heard his voice.

"Anise."

She spun around, her eyes locking with his. He stood just a few feet away, his hand reaching out, pulling her into him. For a moment, time seemed to stand still, the world narrowing until there were only the two of them.

"I've missed you," Duke murmured, his lips brushing against her ear, sending a shiver down her spine.

Anise didn't have the words. She didn't need to. She reached up, cupping his face in her hands, and pulled him down to kiss her. His lips were warm and insistent, and the kiss deepened as she responded with all the pent-up emotion from the past six weeks. The tension that had built between them seemed to melt away, leaving only desire and longing.

Without breaking the kiss, Duke pulled back slightly. "Let's go," he whispered, his voice thick with need.

Anise nodded, her pulse racing. He led her out the backdoor, through the courtyard, and to his car. The drive to the Wilde Building was a blur, their silence only punctuated by quiet glances and the occasional brush of his hand against hers.

When they finally reached his place, the moment they walked in, the tension exploded again. The music from the event still echoed in her head, but the world was reduced to just the two of them—touching, kissing, shedding the layers that had kept them apart.

The night unfolded in a haze of passion, of reconnecting, of finally having what they both desperately craved. Anise felt like she could breathe again, like everything she had been holding back had finally been released.

And in the quiet after, lying next to him with her head resting against his chest, she knew one thing for sure: this—he—was worth every moment of uncertainty.

"When are you going back to the farm studio?" Anise asked in the quiet aftermath.

"Tomorrow," Duke said. "I have three more songs to complete the album. JoJo's is launching their first branch in Montego Bay on Monday. I have to show up."

"Okay, I'm coming with you," Anise said.

Duke sat up in the bed. "What?"

"You heard," Anise said. "I have a fashion expo at the end of the week that I promised Jada I would attend."

"Oh, cool," Duke grinned. "Are you staying until the fashion show is over?"

"I don't know," Anise said. "It depends on how annoying Alyssa is."

Duke laughed. "You know what, I'll take it. This is progress."

Chapter Fourteen

Duke's Ridgeview house was a four-bedroom paradise overlooking a sea view so spectacular that Anise was impressed. Duke had described it, but seeing was believing.

"I would describe this as island luxury," Anise said, walking on the patio after touring the four-bedroom house with ensuite baths. The décor was sophisticated yet inviting, a seamless blend of modern elegance and island charm. Expansive glass doors framed the breathtaking ocean view, letting in the golden glow of the setting sun. Cool, neutral tones accented with touches of deep blue and rich teak wood gave the space a relaxed yet refined feel.

"The décor was clearly chosen by someone with taste," Anise added, running her fingers along the smooth surface of a marble-topped console table.

Duke leaned casually against the patio railing, watching her take it all in. "Glad you approve," he said, his voice warm with amusement. "I wanted something that felt like home but still gave me that vacation vibe."

"You nailed it," she admitted, exhaling as the breeze tousled her curls. "I can see why you love it here."

He studied her for a moment, then pushed off the railing. "Come on," he said, nodding toward the lounge chairs overlooking the sea. "You haven't fully appreciated the place until you've watched the sunset from out here."

After they settled down, Duke turned to her. "So, about the opening of the barbershop tomorrow... You're invited, but my whole family will be there."

Anise inhaled. "Okay."

"Really?" Duke whistled. "The press will be there too."

"I'll come," Anise said.

"I am going to introduce you as my girlfriend," Duke said, "to my family. They'll be staying over here for a couple of days. Deanna and Michael are already in the guest house, so it will be my mom and dad."

"That's fine," Anise murmured.

"I don't know what to say, this is progress," Duke said. "Was it the song?"

"Partly," Anise nodded. "I got the message loud and clear. You said, 'I can't be your secret, Annie; it's breaking your heart.' And partly because I was being a little unreasonable. I think our families, at least, except my mother, should know."

Duke chuckled. "I can work with that. I think it's an open secret anyway. My sister and Alyssa know about us. I told Jairo a couple of months ago he probably told his wife, Audra. Chex knows, which means his wife Garnet knows."

Anise chuckled. "Well then, after tomorrow, that leaves my family. I'll work up to it."

"Now, this is progress," Duke nodded. "You won't mind too badly if I leave you this evening, will you?" he asked, stretching his arms over his head.

She arched a brow. "Oh?"

"I'm due in the studio with DJ Salky," he said, watching her reaction. "He flew in from Nigeria to work on a track with me."

Anise blinked, clearly impressed. "DJ Salky? Afrobeat king DJ Salky?"

Duke nodded, his smirk widening. "The one and only. We locked it in last week. It will be a mix of Afrobeat and R&B—something different, but I'm excited."

"Look at you, international superstar," she said, folding her arms and feigning suspicion. "You didn't mention this before."

"Didn't get a chance," he admitted. "And I knew you'd make that exact face."

Anise laughed. "You mean my impressed-but-trying-to-play-it-cool face?"

"Exactly," Duke teased. "But you don't have to pretend, Anise. I know you're a fan."

She rolled her eyes. "Don't flatter yourself. How about after the session, you come back here for dinner? I'll make all your favorites."

"I am down for that," Duke chuckled. "I missed your cooking. No one can throw down in the kitchen like you."

He reached over and kissed her. "I'll be back in a couple of hours."

Anise nodded.

"Sorry about this," Duke said. "I wanted to be here your first night."

"Don't be," Anise fanned him off. "I knew this was the way it would be while you are working on an album; it's your job."

"You'll have to buy groceries," Duke said. "Some

supermarkets here deliver if you don't want to go into town."

"Noted," Anise said. "Just send me the info, and I'll handle it."

Duke studied her for a moment, his expression softening. "You really don't mind?"

Anise shook her head. "Duke, I knew what I was signing up for. Late-night sessions, last-minute flights, fans pulling you in a million directions—none of this surprises me."

His smirk faded into something more thoughtful. "Still, I don't want you to feel like I'm putting work before you."

She reached up, smoothing a hand over his jaw. "You're not. This is what you do. And when you come back, a home-cooked meal will be waiting for you."

Duke exhaled, a slow smile spreading across his face. "Now that's motivation."

"Good," Anise said, stepping back. "Now go make a hit, superstar."

Duke chuckled, squeezing her hand once before heading for the door. "I'll be back before you know it."

Anise watched him go, shaking her head with a smile. If nothing else, life with Duke was never dull.

****

"**S**omething in here smells good," a voice said behind her.

Anise spun around, forgetting that Alyssa had been living there for a while. She hadn't seen her since she arrived with Duke, and he hadn't mentioned her.

"Hi," she said. "My name is—"

"Anise Crystal," Alyssa nodded. "Annie for short. The secret lover."

"Apparently, that's who I am now," Anise nodded. "I don't know if I'm ever going to live down that song."

Alyssa grabbed a barstool. "Well, it's nice to meet you. You are quite pretty. I kind of get why Duke wouldn't fall for a normal woman with you around."

"I beg your pardon?" Anise raised her eyebrows.

"It's not an insult," Alyssa said hurriedly. "Normal women are the ones like me—the girl-next-door types. Two-parent household, parents still married. My only claim to trauma is Reuben Thomas trying to drunkenly force himself on me at a party. Our type would be classified as normal, uncomplicated, boring, and vanilla.

"You and Madge, on the other hand, are the opposite of normal. You have colorful backgrounds, rotten childhoods, crummy relationships, and crazy stories to tell about famous men flying you out to Paris.

"The not-normal all have extraordinarily pretty faces. They are hunted for their looks and prized for their unique beauty. Even though you are way prettier than Madge. You look much better without all the artifice. She always had on a full face of makeup and ten pounds of hair. It made me think she was hiding something."

Anise smiled. "Thanks. I've been working with the 'less is more' beauty trend. It takes less time to get ready, that's for sure."

"I disliked Madge on sight," Alyssa said. "You may not be as fake, but I still don't like you for Duke."

"Why not?" Anise asked.

"You are damaged," Alyssa said. "Through no fault of your own, your life started off rough. I mean, I can't imagine how bad it was for you. You were a victim of child sex abuse, and I know that was the past, but that sort of thing affects the future and every subsequent relationship you'll have after that. You won't ever be able to love right. The person who messed you up first messed you up for life."

Anise gasped. "You can't say that. How dare you?"

"I didn't come up with it off the top of my head," Alyssa said. "I was reading an article about it. At the time, they were talking about Madge, and I saved it to send to Duke, but they could just as easily be talking about you. You both had the same childhood issues, among other similarities. Let me find it; I saved it in my phone."

Anise stood with her hands on her hips, glaring at Alyssa as she scrolled through her phone.

"Here it is," Alyssa said. "Clinical psychologist Dr. Marlene Whitaker specializes in trauma recovery, and according to her, childhood abuse survivors struggle with intimacy, trust, and forming healthy attachments. Some even sabotage good relationships because, deep down, they don't believe they deserve it. She thinks that's why Madge killed those women—deep down, she didn't think she deserved to be happy. She just had to do something to jeopardize her happy status with Duke."

Anise folded her arms, her jaw tightening. "And you read one article about another woman and decided that's my future?"

Alyssa glanced up from her phone, unfazed. "It's science. And it's not personal. Based on the gossip magazines or entertainment sections of the papers, you change men pretty often. I just don't want Duke getting hurt."

Anise exhaled sharply, trying to steady herself. "That's very noble of you, Alyssa, but you don't know me. You don't know how much work I've done to heal, how much therapy I've had, or how I navigate my relationships. So no, I won't let you or some article decide my capabilities."

Alyssa studied her for a long moment, then nodded slowly. "Fair enough. But you're still on trial in my book. I can't overlook the fact that you didn't want anyone to know you were dating Duke, and you're willing to let someone else have his baby. You don't seem like you're in it for the long haul."

Anise let out a dry laugh. "You are making too many assumptions about me and Duke. And you're acting way too knowledgeable about my life for someone I just met."

"You put your life out there," Alyssa shrugged. "You are the poster child for TMI. Telling your story is a blessing and a curse. Complete strangers feel as if they know you, and who can blame them? I watched all of your interviews on Claire Talk. It somewhat gave me some perspective on the way you think."

"You have no idea how I think," Anise sighed. "I get it. You have a crush on Duke and resent any woman in his life."

"No, you don't get it," Alyssa said passionately. "I have loved Duke Jones since I knew what love was. And he has never shown me the least bit of interest—except for one night when he was drunk, but that's another story. I got over my feelings a while ago when I realized I'm not his type. You can't help who you love, and he doesn't love normal. I get that.

"I want to experience love someday with someone who loves me back, so I know Duke is off the table. Does it sting a little? I guess. He's handsome, he's famous, he's decent, and he was the topic of all my childhood fantasies.

"So, to counter your assumption about me," Alyssa continued, "I'm not jealous of you or Madge. You are not normal women who have had normal life experiences. I would be jealous if he was dating someone from a stable home with a clean past and comparable to our upbringing."

Anise gasped. "Okay, then."

"It's just facts," Alyssa said. "Despite Duke's stardom,

he was brought up in a loving two-parent household. You, Madge, and women of your ilk have no clue what a normal family looks like. It baffles me greatly why he is even remotely attracted to women like you—broken, damaged women whose moral compass is so far out there that one of them is in prison for murder. You almost went for attempted murder."

"My case is different from Madge's by far," Anise said, incensed. "I caught my ex-husband doing inappropriate things to our toddlers. I wasn't thinking straight at the time. What mother in her right mind wouldn't have gotten upset enough to do something about it?"

"I know," Alyssa said. "And I applaud you for making sure he was punished for his actions. But if you hadn't missed the shot, you would have been the one behind bars. I'm just saying. And your kids would have grown up without you, and who knows? They may have become just as damaged as you."

Anise sighed. "Your comparisons of me to Madge is somewhat justified. We did have a tough start to life, but I will not accept someone I don't know judging my moral compass as being that far out there."

Alyssa looked at her assessingly. "You won't stay with Duke. You'll ditch him like a hot potato when the going gets rough, or you'll find some excuse to leave when things get too permanent or emotional. At the first sign of adversity— or maybe even now—you're already thinking of a way to ditch him. The least excuse you get, you're gone."

"Goodness," Anise murmured. "I have never felt so piled on in my life, and my mother is Rosemary Ruby, the author of the book How to Gaslight Anise at Every Opportunity. For your information, Duke and I have been together for close to three years now."

"Three years in secret," Alyssa shrugged. "That doesn't count. You mean he sleeps over now and again, you have clandestine dates, and you giggle together because the world doesn't know about you two. Fair enough, but that's not a true relationship. People having affairs do what you do all the time.

"Even though Duke seems to choose your type, he's still a traditional sort and doesn't like living like that. That's why he wifed up Madge so quickly and wants to marry you and have a family. But you can't turn a ho into a housewife."

"Now listen," Anise narrowed her eyes at Alyssa. "I am finished with this conversation."

"Of course you would be," Alyssa said knowingly. "No one has ever bluntly told you things you don't want to hear."

Anise laughed dryly. "You have not met my mother."

"And I guess when Duke comes home, you're going to tell him to ask me to leave," Alyssa smirked. "You can't handle opposition in any way, can you?"

"I will not tell him to ask you to leave," Anise said. "I would tell you myself. I am this close to throwing you out."

Alyssa nodded. "I knew you were thin-skinned. You'd probably throw my stuff off the top floor and scream like a madwoman—all because you can't handle opposition or the truth."

Anise bit her lip. She had indeed envisioned doing something like that while Alyssa talked, but she refused to give this woman the reaction she was so clearly goading her into.

Inhaling deeply, she said calmly, "I am not thin-skinned. I just like peace, and you are not a peaceful person. You came in here attacking me about my relationship with Duke. I have every right not to want you around. I can't recall being so insulted in my life."

"I didn't insult you," Alyssa said.

"You called me a ho—short for whore. I take exception to that," Anise said. "And I can assure you, I've seen plenty of whores turned into housewives and plenty of housewives who are whores. Their marriages last, and they do just fine."

"But you and Duke won't last," Alyssa said. "Your relationship hasn't been tested. You've operated in secret so far, and there's been no opportunity for any real roadblocks. But the cracks are showing. He sang Secret Love as a cry for help. You heard the line, 'I can't be your secret, Annie, it's breaking my heart.' You are breaking his heart."

Alyssa got up. "Well, I guess I can't expect to get any of your food after this chat. But I'll leave you with a question: What would you do if you had a friend like Duke from childhood, and he kept showing up with women like you and Madge? Would you accept that this is just the way it is—that he will choose your type of woman, get hurt, and then start the process all over again? Or would you do something about it to make sure he doesn't get hurt again?"

"Do something like what?" Anise frowned.

"You'll see," Alyssa said mysteriously.

"Are you threatening me?" Anise asked, narrowing her eyes.

"No," Alyssa said. "It may not seem like it now, but I like you. When I first met Madge, I hated her on sight—and that was when she was at her phony friendliest. I just couldn't warm to her. But you? I have mixed feelings about you."

She left the kitchen, and Anise stared after her, feeling thoroughly unsettled. Alyssa had been abrasive, rude, and judgmental, but she had also been eerily perceptive. Anise's mind replayed the conversation, each cutting remark lodging itself deeper.

What on earth was Alyssa planning to do?

Chapter Fifteen

Anise did not get to complain about Alyssa to Duke or say much of anything to him the day after. He had gotten in late, crawled into bed in the early hours of the morning, and woken up to shower while she was still half-asleep. She had vaguely heard him take a phone call before he disappeared.

She glanced at the bedside clock—it was a little after eight. Usually, she didn't sleep in this late but there was something about Ridgeview that made her want to. Last night, she had left the balcony door open, turned off the AC, and let the fresh air lull her to sleep. She had spent half the night tossing and turning, wondering if she was really as abnormal and damaged as Alyssa had suggested. Eventually, exhaustion had won, and she had drifted into a fitful sleep—until Duke had come in at two and thrown himself onto the bed.

Had she told him that Alyssa was evil? She couldn't remember.

Sighing, she got out of bed.

They had never had this type of situation to navigate—him coming in late from the studio, trying to finish up an album, her staying home, cooking, and waiting for him. Alyssa was snarky and completely inappropriate, but some things she had said were correct.

Duke and her had never really been tested.

Anise stretched, then made quick work of a cold shower, washing her hair. She decided to leave it down in a wash-and-go. Her hair now reached almost to her butt, streaked with several strands of gray that she had dyed brown. Maybe one day, she'd try a more exciting color.

As she applied light makeup, she called Jada. She still had no idea when the barbershop launch was—she had never asked.

"Hey," she said when her friend answered. "How's it going?"

"Quite well," Jada gushed. "Did you know that all your girls said yes to coming to Montego Bay and participating in the bridal show for me? Bless their pretty little hearts."

"They said yes?" Anise was surprised. "What did Grandma Saidie say?"

"She said she's been wanting to take a vacation for ages," Jada chuckled. "And as a woman who's never been married, she said it would be her honor to rock a wedding dress—at least she could pretend for a while that she was a girl again with her whole future ahead of her."

"I can't believe it," Anise whispered. "What did you promise them?"

"Nothing," Jada snorted. "As for your dress, I finished it last night. It's gorgeous. I'll need you to do a fitting for me. I'll be in Ridgeview by Thursday."

"Let's hope I'm still here," Anise said. "Because I am very close to going into hibernation mode and curling up somewhere quiet for a while."

"No," Jada whispered. "What happened? What did Duke do?"

"Nothing. It's his friend Alyssa who's the issue," Anise said. "She called me abnormal, said Duke was only attracted to troubled women. She compared me to Madge, said Duke and I haven't really been tested, and at the first real challenge, I'm going to run because I can't have a stable relationship—I'm damaged for life."

Jada gasped. "Is she a psychologist or something?"

"No," Anise grunted. "I think she's a realtor. She made me so mad yesterday. But… what if she's right? My track record speaks for itself. I'm thinking of packing my bags and returning to Kingston so I don't have to face Duke's family at the barbershop opening today. What if they all think like her? I mean, Madge and I do share similar stories if you think about it."

"Stop it right there," Jada said firmly. "You are not Madge, and you never will be. Madge knowingly killed three women—befriended them and then poisoned them. That is not you. That's a special kind of evil. And yes, superficially, you may have been similarly abused as children, but unfortunately, a lot of women in this country can say that. I was almost raped when I was nine."

"You were? How?" Anise asked, stunned.

"I had a pervert neighbor when I lived with my mom. One day, he peered his head over the wall and offered me some plums from a basket. You should have seen them, Anise. They were red and juicy-looking. He dangled them over the fence and told me I'd have to come around to get them.

"I was just about to go through the gate when another neighbor passed by, saw me heading toward his place, and said he was coming with me.

"You should have seen the disappointment on that perv's face when he saw me with company. He handed me the plums, and my other neighbor walked me back, warning me never to go over there alone again.

"He even woke my mother—who was knackered from a late shift at the hospital—and told her to be more vigilant because the guy next door liked young girls. I'll never forget the scared look in my mother's eyes when he said that. So many young, trusting girls were never fortunate enough to have a neighbor passing by at just the right moment."

"Oh, wow," Anise whispered, shaken.

"I said all of that to say," Jada continued, "that you cannot allow anyone and everyone to define you by your past. You are not broken, and you are not doomed to fail in relationships. You are a survivor, and you've built something real with Duke. Don't let some bitter woman with her own issues make you question yourself."

Anise exhaled slowly, staring at herself in the mirror. She wanted to believe Jada—she really did. But Alyssa's words still clung to her like a shadow.

"I don't know, Jada," she admitted. "I just feel like maybe I'm not cut out for this. Maybe Alyssa can see something I can't."

"Girl, please," Jada scoffed. "Alyssa is projecting her own nonsense onto you. You've got a good man, a good life. And yeah, this is the first time you and Duke are really navigating something like this, but every couple has to go through it. It doesn't mean you're doomed. It just means you're learning."

Anise bit her lip. Maybe Jada was right. Maybe she was overthinking.

"Anyway," Jada continued, "don't you dare run back to Kingston. I'll be in Ridgeview by Thursday. I fully expect to see you here, standing strong and making Alyssa eat her words just by existing."

Anise laughed despite herself. "Alright, alright. No running—yet."

"Good. Now go out there, look fabulous, and remind these people who you are."

After hanging up, Anise took a deep breath and squared her shoulders. She wasn't going to let Alyssa's words ruin her day. Duke was her man. Ridgeview was her temporary home. And if Alyssa wanted a fight—well… Anise could hold her own.

****

The kitchen was filled with people when she went downstairs. Well, it seemed like a lot.

Duke saw her before she could bolt back upstairs. "Everyone, this is Anise," he said to the room at large. "My girlfriend."

"Anise, this is my family. My dad, John Jones."

John waved at her while talking on the phone. He was a big guy with a bit of a belly—an older version of Duke.

"My mom, Yvette Jones."

Yvette was a stylish-looking woman with the lushest sister locks Anise had ever seen. She stepped away from the stove, where she seemed to be preparing a feast, and warmly hugged Anise.

"I've always wanted to meet you, Anise," Yvette said. "What would you like for breakfast? I decided to go full Jamaican today—green bananas, boiled dumplings, ackee, and saltfish."

She smiled at her warmly.

"I'll have that," Anise said with a grateful smile. "Thanks."

"No problem." Yvette nodded.

"My sister Deanna and her husband, Michael—who is Alyssa's brother," Duke said, pointing to the two people. Both of them were on the phone.

Deanna, a pretty, shapely version of Duke, smiled and waved. She covered the mouthpiece of her phone. "I've always wanted to meet you too, Anise Crystal."

Anise smiled, relieved to hear that.

"Me too," Michael said. He grinned and gave her a thumbs-up. He was tall and muscular, the kind of man who clearly took working out seriously. "When we have some downtime, I want to pick your brain about winemaking. I absolutely have to know what goes on behind the scenes."

"It's his latest hobby," Deanna chuckled. "All of his efforts so far have been below par."

They went back to their respective conversations.

Duke took Anise's hand and led her to the nook where Jairo was sitting with his daughter in his arms.

"My cousin Jairo and his newborn, Jai," Duke introduced.

"Hi, Anise," Jairo said. "This little girl thrives on chaos. Look how happy she is to be among the noise and mayhem. Next door was too quiet for her—she made such a fuss that her mother told me to take her out. So we ended up here in Jones Town, where the noise level is right up her alley."

"How old is she?" Anise whispered, gazing at the perfect, miniature beauty. "What a pretty baby."

"Eight weeks," Jairo replied. "Want to hold her?"

"Of course," Anise said. "I love the scent of babies."

Jairo handed Jai to Anise, and she cradled the tiny girl gently in her arms. Jai's big, curious eyes blinked up at her before she made a small, contented sigh and snuggled closer.

"She likes you," Jairo noted with a grin.

Anise smiled, inhaling the soft, powdery scent of the baby.

"She's so sweet. She looks just like you."

Jairo chuckled. "Both my children look like me. I challenged Audra to have another one to see where the genetics will land next. She says she's considering it."

Anise chuckled. "Don't tell me she's falling for that?"

Jairo smirked. "She says she's considering it."

Duke watched Anise, his eyes softening as she held the baby. He reached over and brushed a strand of hair from her face. "You look good like that," he murmured, just for her to hear.

Anise glanced up at him, warmth flooding her cheeks. She wasn't sure how to respond to that, so she just smiled and focused on Jai, who let out a tiny yawn.

"So, Anise," Yvette called from the stove, "how long are you staying in Ridgeview? Are we finally going to get to know you properly?"

Anise hesitated. The truth was, she hadn't decided yet. With Alyssa's words still lingering in her mind, part of her wanted to retreat—to put space between herself and this new world Duke was trying to pull her into. But another part of her—the part that felt the weight of his gaze, the warmth of his family, and the unexpected comfort of holding Jai— wanted to stay.

She glanced at Duke, who raised an eyebrow in silent question.

"I'm…not sure yet," she admitted, shifting Jai slightly in her arms. "But I guess we'll see."

Yvette nodded as if she understood more than Anise was saying. "Take your time and process things," she said, returning to the stove. Then, after a pause, she added, "Life is like this pot of ackee and saltfish. Sometimes sweet, sometimes salty, always a mix of things you didn't expect. But if you let it cook long enough, the flavors work together in a way you never imagined."

Anise blinked, absorbing the words.

Yvette smiled knowingly. "You don't have to have it all figured out today, Anise. Just don't be so quick to turn off the fire before the dish is done."

Duke glanced at his mother, then at Anise, as if waiting to see how she would take it.

Anise let out a small breath and nodded. "I'll try to remember that."

"Good," Yvette said, plating up the food. "Now eat. Thinking too much on an empty stomach never did anybody any good."

Chapter Sixteen

Alyssa watched as the Jones family befriended Anise Crystal. It was the same scenario with Madge all over again. They were being their warm, accepting selves without properly vetting a potentially serious relationship of Duke's. It was like they had forgotten what happened with Madge.

She stuck her head around the corner and greeted them cheerily. "I wish I could stay, but I have an early meeting with a colleague. See you all later at the opening."

They waved her off, and she drove to the office, wondering why she had taken it upon herself to save Duke from another calamitous relationship. Maybe because she had seen him at his worst when Madge had proven to be a murderous liar, she didn't want to see him there again when Anise inevitably did the same.

But how did she know that Anise would be the same? She had tested her the other evening, and the woman had shown remarkable restraint. Alyssa had said some pretty hurtful things, and Anise had kept her cool for the most part.

She needed to come up with another plan.

Duke was a crazy-woman magnet.

She parked in the school lot and scrolled through her phone, searching for ways to test someone in a relationship to see if they would last as a couple. Alyssa tapped her fingers against the steering wheel as she skimmed through the search results. Most were about compatibility quizzes, deep conversation topics, and subtle red flags to watch for in a relationship. None of it felt quite right. She needed something more… real. Something that would push Anise into showing her true colors.

Madge had seemed perfect at first, too. Sweet, charming, even doting. Until she wasn't.

Alyssa exhaled sharply and tossed her phone onto the passenger seat. Maybe she was overthinking this. Maybe Duke had actually learned from his past mistakes. But then again, hadn't he looked just as smitten with Anise as he had with Madge?

The more she thought about Anise, the more she was convinced that history would repeat itself. There was no way Anise wasn't hiding some major character flaw. People like her—with her background—didn't just become perfect or even passable partners without a deeper, darker side waiting to unfold.

Or was she being fanciful? And why did this matter so much?

A tiny part of her—a mere dot—wished that Duke would love her as much as he had loved Madge and now Anise. And that little part of her didn't want to see him hurt again.

She reached for her phone again when her colleague, Nakia Sanders, knocked on her window. Alyssa jumped.

"Are you coming to the meeting or what?" Nakia asked

nasally.

"I'm coming," Alyssa mumbled.

Nakia had been cozying up to her all week after hearing that there would be a JoJo's in Montego Bay and a grand opening, which meant that DJ Duke would be there. Everybody knew JoJo's was Duke's family business. And if ever there was a rabid fan, Nakia was it. She dreamed of ways to get closer to Duke. It was usually annoying to listen to her fawn over him. Ever since she discovered that Alyssa was close to the family, she was suddenly on her radar.

Nakia was also another damaged one—she ran away from home at fourteen to live with her boyfriend, who trafficked her to his rich friends. She had finally escaped and made something of her life, which was a plus.

Nakia fancied herself a singer and actress and had just wrapped up a popular stage play in which she had a lead role. Alyssa had gone to one installment and had found it tedious. Nakia had more enthusiasm than talent. And she was pretty. People tended to overlook weaknesses when a girl had her looks.

Nakia was the kind of girl Duke would find attractive. She was slim yet curvy, wore long hair extensions, and always had her nails done. She had a couple of tattoos and body piercings. In fact, the more Alyssa looked at her, the more she realized Nakia had more than a passing resemblance to Madge.

An idea was forming in Alyssa's head.

It was too wonderful not to pursue.

Maybe she could use Nakia's resemblance to Madge as an advantage. The perfect test of Duke and Anise's relationship began percolating in her mind.

It was invasive. It could be hurtful. It might make Duke mad and not talk to her for a while.

But it would answer the question: What was the breaking point of Duke and Anise's relationship?

How would she arrange it? Alyssa thought feverishly.

She opened her car door and called to Nakia, who was almost at the entrance to the building. "Hey, girl!" she said, projecting her friendliest persona.

Nakia stopped.

Alyssa smiled widely. She felt fake, but she had to do this. It was for Duke.

****

"**O**h my God, DJ Duke! You are my favorite artiste of all time!"

A woman was following him around, staring at him adoringly.

"I used to hang out at Right Vibes Studio just so I could get a glimpse of you," she said breathlessly when he finally stopped and looked around for Anise.

"I wanted to break into the music business at one time. I even entered that competition to be one of your backup singers, but I didn't get through. You saw me crying in the parking lot, and we chatted a little. Then you signed an autograph for me. It said, Keep your head up, Nakia. Never give up. Whenever I'm down, I read it. Don't you remember me?"

He vaguely remembered something like that. Duke smiled, mainly because she had looked a lot like Madge, and it had taken him aback.

"I do remember. How are you doing these days?"

"Much better," Nakia chuckled. "I finally got the message that maybe music wasn't my thing when I got booed off stage at a free concert. So, I decided to get my real estate license. But I still act in local productions, and I'm a good dancer. It seems like I'm a bit better at that."

"Your friend Alyssa and I work at the same company—just different branches."

"DJ Duke," a photographer called from behind them. "Can I get a picture with you and your latest girlfriend?"

"She's not my girlfriend," Duke said, turning around. "But you can get a picture."

The photographer smiled and took the photo. "You definitely have a type, DJ Duke."

No doubt, by tomorrow, the papers would claim Nakia was his secret love. Anise would probably like that it wasn't her they were speculating about.

Where was she?

"Excuse me a second, Nakia," he said, finally spotting Anise holding court with a few women—including his mother, who had seamlessly accepted Anise into his life as if she had always been there.

Anise was laughing at something one of them said.

"Hey, you good?" he asked, slipping an arm around her waist.

She glanced up at him, a smile playing on her lips. "I'm fine. Yvette was just telling us about her exploits as a barber when your father had the flu for a few weeks. Your father was almost out of a job when he got back."

"True," Duke nodded. "Mom can cut hair almost as good as Dad."

"He has to say almost," Yvette said, "for John's sake."

The women laughed, and Duke couldn't help but grin. His mother made everyone feel at home, and Anise was clearly fitting in seamlessly. It was a nice feeling. He let himself enjoy it—for the moment.

Hopefully, this was one step closer to the two of them

making a permanent commitment to each other.
A man could hope.

Chapter Seventeen

It had been a good week, Anise thought with satisfaction. Duke's family had spent a few days, and they were fun. Even Alyssa seemed as if she had done a complete one-eighty in personality. She was pleasant and cordial in their rare meetups.

"You want to be in my music video with DJ Salky?" Duke asked Anise on Thursday morning while they were eating breakfast together. It was their only real one-on-one time lately. He worked late into the night, and until late yesterday evening, his family had been around.

"You just did the song, and now you're doing a video?" Anise raised her eyebrows. "How come?"

"Because Salky is here for a limited time," Duke said. "We're just doing everything while he's here. Besides, I think this song will blow up. It's nice to drop the video for social media at the same time."

"Cool," Anise said. "What's the name of the song?"

"Tried and True," Duke chuckled. "The lyrics are epic. I wrote it with you in mind."

"Really?" Anise groaned. "Another one? Did you call me Annie again?"

"Nope," Duke chuckled.

"Sing it for me," Anise said.

Duke wiped his mouth with a napkin and leaned back in his chair, smirking. "You really want me to sing it right now?"

Anise popped a piece of toast into her mouth and nodded. "Why not? You're always claiming your songs are fire."

Duke laughed. "They usually are."

Anise smiled. "I concede that."

Duke sipped his coffee, set the cup down, and tapped a rhythm on the table. His voice was smooth when he started singing:

"Late nights, long roads, still you're by my side,
Through every storm, through every fight.
We've had our doubts, we've had our fears,
But love don't break, not after all these years.

I'll never cheat on you, never walk away,
Through the fire, through the rain, I'm here to stay.
They can test us, they can try to break us in two,
But if we are tested, we are tried and true."

Anise bit her lip to hide her smile. It was good.

Duke watched her reaction, his lips twitching. "You like it."

"It's okay," she said, pretending nonchalance.

"Okay?" Duke scoffed. "That's not what your face is saying."

Anise huffed. "Fine, it's good. Very good."

Duke grinned. "So, are you in?"

"For the video?" Anise hesitated. "I don't think so."

Duke leaned forward. "Come on, Anise. The song is about us."

She sighed. "What would I have to do?"

"Nothing crazy. It's a simple concept. The setting would be at one of Chex's guest houses. I'd be heading to work, and you'd be sitting at home looking pretty. DJ Salky is my friend who comes to check on me when I'm gone, and you answer. He makes a move on you, and you tell him no. I double back home and find you kicking him out."

Anise sighed. "Sounds good, but I can't act to save my life. I'd be too self-conscious. It's not my thing."

"I knew it was a long shot," Duke chuckled. "I told the guys I would ask Anise Crystal to star as my love interest, and they all said I would strike out."

"The guys know me better than you," Anise teased. "Besides, I am your love interest in real life."

Duke smiled. "It was worth a shot." He leaned back. "Well then, the hunt begins for the love interest. I guess Kenan, the director, already contacted the agencies."

"When is the video going to be shot?" Anise asked.

"Today," Duke said. "I think I'll sleep over at Chex's. Filming will go way into the night. You'll see me on Friday morning."

"Okay," Anise said. "I might spend the night next door then."

"With Jairo and Audra?" Duke asked.

"No, silly," Anise said. "With Jada. She's moving into the house next door today. Richard wants a reconciliation, and she agreed to a trial."

"So your best friend will be next door?" Duke grinned. "What are the odds that you may not want to go back to

Kingston?"

"We can split our time between here and Kingston," Anise said. "With the highway, the journey is much shorter than before."

Duke nodded. "True. I was thinking the same thing."

"Good morning, lovely people." Alyssa breezed into the kitchen, smiling widely. "How are you folks?"

"Good," Duke smiled. "What has you so positive this morning?"

"My course has reached its halfway mark." Alyssa grinned. "And I made a sale at the crack of dawn! It was a customer I was playing the long game with, and he finally decided to buy."

"Good for you," Anise said pleasantly. She still did not trust Alyssa, but she had been next to invisible these last few days.

"That's great," Duke said. "You should celebrate your win."

"I intend to," Alyssa smiled. "I may take Nakia to lunch today."

"Nakia?" Duke raised an eyebrow.

"You remember Nakia," Alyssa said, filling her cup with coffee. "She was the girl I saw you talking to at the store opening."

"Oh yes," Duke nodded. "She said she tried out to be my backup singer a couple of years ago and didn't get through."

"Yes, that's her," Alyssa said. "She does some modeling and acting on the side. She's quite pretty, don't you think?"

Duke nodded. "She is."

"She looks a lot like Madge, too." Alyssa's eyes connected with Anise's, a knowing little smirk in them.

Anise looked away. What was she up to? Was she trying to make her insecure? Well, it wasn't working.

Her phone rang. It was Cinnamon. They usually chatted in the morning before Cinnamon went to work.

"Hey, Firstborn," she greeted her daughter and got up. "Excuse me a moment."

When she left the kitchen, Alyssa went over and sat in front of Duke.

"I mention Nakia because she has been hounding me to ask if she could be in one of your music videos."

Duke nodded. "Okay. Tell me about her."

"She can dance, sing, act, model." Alyssa shrugged. "She does everything. She's always entering competitions and contests. She is determined to be in front of the cameras in whatever capacity she can. Real estate is just her backup plan. She always says she's quitting as soon as she makes it."

Duke chuckled. "She sounds interesting."

"I knew you'd think so," Alyssa said. "So what should I tell her?"

"Tell her to come by the studio today. We're going to shoot a video this evening. If Kenan, the director, is impressed with her, she's in."

"Yay for her." Alyssa got up. "I have to go. I'm running a bit late."

****

"So, where were we?" Anise asked after coming back into the kitchen from her call.

"You were going to beg me to marry you and give you some babies," Duke said, getting up and pulling her closer.

Anise chuckled. "I'm warming up to that."

"Really?" Duke whispered into her hair, his hands sliding

down her back in a slow, possessive caress. "How warm are we talking?"

Anise tilted her head, her lips brushing the side of his neck. "Hmm… still preheating."

Duke chuckled, his grip tightening around her waist. "I can work with that." He lifted her onto the counter, stepping between her legs as his fingers traced lazy circles on her thighs.

Anise sighed, her body melting into his touch. "You're real confident, huh?"

"Always," Duke murmured, his lips skimming along her jawline. "Especially when it comes to you."

She bit her lip, her fingers tangling in his hair as he kissed the corner of her mouth—teasing, waiting. Her pulse quickened.

"I could keep you here all day," he said huskily, his lips finally capturing hers, slow and deep.

Anise exhaled against him, her hands sliding down his chest, feeling the steady beat of his heart beneath her fingertips. "You'd love that, wouldn't you?"

Duke smirked. "More than anything." He nipped at her bottom lip, making her shiver. "But I want the whole thing, Anise. Not just stolen moments in the kitchen."

She stilled, her breath catching. The heat between them wasn't just physical—it never had been.

Duke cupped her face, his thumb brushing over her cheek. "I want you. All of you. No half-measures."

Anise swallowed hard, her heart pounding. "You already have me, Duke."

His eyes searched hers, dark and intense. "Then stop fighting it."

She pulled him closer, pressing her forehead to his. "I'm not fighting. I'm just making sure."

Duke kissed her again, this time softer, slower. "Then let me prove it."

Anise closed her eyes, surrendering to the way he made her feel—wanted, cherished, his.

Chapter Eighteen

Jada called just as Duke left for the studio.

"I'm next door, just drove in. Please come over—and bring food with you. I'm starving."

Anise chuckled. She hurriedly showered and pulled on her comfiest leggings and a tight top. She was literally glowing—Duke was good for her. She pulled her hair back into a high ponytail and inspected her makeup-free face in the mirror.

Not bad for forty-two.

She looked at least a decade younger than her age. She could pull off having young children again without being mistaken for their grandmother.

She chuckled to herself. She was on the verge of making a huge commitment to Duke—she could feel it. Her life was on the cusp of a significant change. She couldn't believe that she, Anise Crystal Cooper—the girl voted least likely to have a normal life—was actually in contention for what would pass for one.

Granted, her boyfriend was a sought-after musician, popular and loved by the ladies, but he had been married before. And through no fault of his own, that marriage had ended. She knew how to handle Duke's fame. She was secure in their relationship—that made all the difference in the world.

She grabbed her phone and headed to the kitchen, putting together a quick plate for Jada—leftover grilled chicken, a fresh salad, and some garlic bread. It was simple but would be satisfying. As she packed it up, her thoughts kept circling back to Duke.

It wasn't just about love. She had loved before. Had been hurt before. But this was different. It was solid, steady. A choice she wanted to make, not one she felt pressured into.

Carrying the food next door, she was surprised to see Jada sitting in her vehicle, watching as a young woman—around Sage's age—directed an army of workmen carrying furniture through the house.

"That's Kendrea, the interior designer," Jada said. "Richard told her last night that I wanted to stay in the guest house. Always absentminded, our Richard," she added sarcastically. "But I can't believe he accomplished all this. This place is glorious."

"It really is," Anise agreed.

"So, how's it going?" Jada grinned. "Tell me all about your week. You met Duke's family; they liked you, and the world didn't fall apart."

Anise nodded. "Yup. I was worried for nothing. I'm thinking that I should introduce him to the girls and Grandma Saidie when they get here."

"Cinnamon said they're traveling together and booked a hotel rooms for the weekend."

"Yes," Jada nodded. "They all agreed to help me out—bless their hearts. I'm happy that things are working out for you and Duke. You'll see it in its glory as soon as we have a place to hang the dress. Maybe you'll even wear it one day soon—for real. It's yours after you model it for me tomorrow."

Anise smiled. "Thank you. Now I can't wait to see it."

"Mrs. Tinsdale?" Kendrea walked over. "Is there anything specific you'd like me to add to the décor to make you feel more at home?"

Jada giggled. "Nobody has called me Mrs. Tinsdale in so long, I almost looked over my shoulder to see if Richard's mom was here. You can call me Jada and this is my friend, Anise."

Kendrea smiled. "Nice to meet you, Anise."

"Likewise," Anise nodded. "I saw what you did with Duke and Jairo's place—you're really good at what you do."

"Thank you," Kendrea nodded. "I had input from both clients when I was decorating. Richard told me to make this place pretty and that your favorite color was red."

"Aww," Jada grinned. "He remembered! But it's my favorite clothing color, not interior design color. I wouldn't want the walls slathered in red."

"Thankfully," Kendrea chuckled, "they're now a nice, neutral sandy beige. I was thinking of working with that so we don't have to deal with paint fumes, and I'd bring in pops of red and brown with cushions and rugs."

"How long will this take?" Jada asked.

"It's only two bedrooms," Kendrea said. "Luckily, I anticipated working on this place already. I designed four of the five main houses here and all the guesthouses. I went with different designs for each. I had a plan in mind for this one just in case Richard wanted me to do some staging, and I reserved some furniture at the warehouse where I get my pieces. So, if everything goes according to plan, we should have it all wrapped up by tonight."

Jada let out a low whistle. "That's impressive. I was expecting to be crashing on Anise's couch for at least a week."

"No need for that," Kendrea said. "Your room will be ready."

"Cool," Jada sighed. "Can I wheel in my wedding dresses? I want them upright and uncreased—I have an expo tomorrow."

"Give me a moment," Kendrea said. "I'll check on the movers and see where they are."

"Tell you what," Jada said. "Don't bother—I don't want them to be in your way. I'll go to Anise's place to eat and hang out, then I'll return around six."

"That would be perfect," Kendrea said. "We can pull off amazing things by then—I'll even have the cleaning service come in."

****

"So," Jada said when they were situated on the patio at Duke's house, "tell me what's really going on with you and Duke? You're glowing, Anise. Don't even try to deny it."

Anise laughed, setting her glass of iced tea down. "I am not glowing. That's just good skincare and a full night's sleep."

"Uh-huh," Jada smirked. "Sure it is."

Anise rolled her eyes but couldn't fight the smile tugging at her lips. "Okay, fine. Things are… good. Better than good."

Jada leaned in, eyes twinkling. "So, spill. Are we talking about moving in together good? Wedding bells good? Baby-making good?"

Anise hesitated for a beat before sighing. "Honestly? I think I want it all with him, Jada. Marriage, a home, kids."

Jada's eyes widened. "Wait. Are you serious?"

"Yeah," Anise admitted, a little breathless now that she'd actually said it out loud. "I said I was done with all that, but with Duke… I don't know. It feels different. Feels right. My therapist said I should trust my instincts. This is me trusting them, for once."

Jada sat back, grinning like she'd just won the lottery. "Oh, girl. You are in deep."

Anise laughed, but there was no denying it. "Yeah. I really am."

They hung out for the day, chatting and laughing, before finally dragging themselves next door at sunset.

The frantic activity at the front was over. Only Kendrea was inside, and the place smelled subtly sweet. There was a bouquet of red roses on the center table.

"A nod to your love of red," Kendrea said to Jada when they stepped in.

"It's really nice." Jada nodded.

"You are a miracle worker," Anise whistled. "Out of chaos, you created cohesion."

Kendrea looked up. "I had loads of help. They recently left. Do you guys need help removing the wedding dresses from the car?"

"Yes, please," Jada said, looking pleased. "I can't wait for Anise to try on the dress."

They helped Jada remove her dresses from the car. She had even carried a sewing machine in case she needed to make adjustments.

Anise went to try on the gold and white creation as soon as Jada pointed to it.

The moment Anise slipped into the dress, she felt its

weight settle around her—luxurious and elegant. The gold embroidery shimmered under the soft lighting, intricate patterns catching every flicker of movement. She smoothed her hands over the bodice, the fitted top accentuating her curves before cascading into a flowing skirt. It was stunning.

She turned to the full-length mirror and let out a slow breath. "Wow."

Jada clapped her hands together, eyes shining. "I knew it! You look amazing."

Kendrea stepped closer, tilting her head as she assessed the fit. "It's perfect. I would like you to do a dress for me. I'm getting married in a couple of months."

"Oh, really? Congrats." Anise twisted and turned in the mirror. "It feels so light. I love it."

Jada smiled.

"When Richard called me a few days ago and said I should drop everything I was doing to work on the guest house because his estranged wife was coming into town, I had no idea you were the famous Jada, the dress designer. My sister, Kenice, tried to get you to do her wedding dress, but you were booked solid."

"Oh, I was." Jada nodded. "Tell her sorry."

"It was a couple of years ago," Kendrea chuckled, "but you are talented, and this dress looks amazing on Anise who has a fabulous shape."

"Thank you." Anise smiled. "So, when are you getting married?"

Kendrea nodded. "Summer. We pushed the wedding date back until later this year because my fiancé wants to get married at his ideal weight."

"That's unique," Jada said. "Brides are usually the ones getting fit for their wedding."

Kendrea nodded. "Well, he lost a ton of weight and wants

to show it off."

"That's awesome," Anise said. "Kudos to him."

"I'll tell him," Kendrea nodded. "And since you both are staying over here, you may be able to tell him yourself. We live here at Ridgeview. I've been thinking that we need a neighborhood party of some sort so we can get to know our neighbors better."

"I doubt I'll be staying long enough for a neighborhood party," Jada said. "I'm here for the expo and a supposed trial period with Richard, but he texted me just now and said he's off to the Bahamas for a few days. He has a housing project there, and his attention is urgently needed."

"Richard is a workaholic," Kendrea said. "When I tell him he needs to slow down, he says work helps him with his loneliness."

Jada looked taken aback. "I expected that he would have a girlfriend or something."

"I work with Richard on staging his houses," Kendrea said, "and I have never seen him look at another woman. He doesn't flirt; he's not overly familiar with anyone. The man is about business and that alone. I was genuinely shocked to hear he had a wife when he told me a year ago."

"Our story is a tad complicated," Jada let out a dry laugh. "But here I am." She shook her head. "I have no idea why he even asked me to come. If he was just going off to the Bahamas, what's the point?"

Kendrea shrugged. "Maybe he wanted to see if you'd actually show up. Or maybe he thought he could handle seeing you again, then panicked and fled."

Jada's lips pressed together. "Well, if that's the case, he wasted our time."

Anise shot her a look. "Come on, Jada. You knew this was never going to be simple."

Jada sighed. "You're right. I just..." She trailed off, smoothing an imaginary wrinkle in her dress. "I expected him to at least be here if he was serious about this trial period."

Kendrea folded her arms. "Richard doesn't do anything without a reason. If he left, it's because he really had to."

Jada nodded slowly. "Maybe. But it doesn't change the fact that I have no idea where I stand with him."

"Well, let's not dwell," Anise said. "You need to prep for the expo. Aren't we supposed to be decorating your booth? Tonight is going to be a long night."

Jada exhaled and forced a smile. "You're right. Business first. Feelings later."

Kendrea chuckled. "That sounds like something Richard himself would say. I'll leave you ladies to it. You'll see me around—I have the main house to design. It will not take me as short a time as this."

After Kendrea left, Jada looked at Anise. "You can't mess this up with Duke, Anise. You have his full attention whenever you want. That's a luxury I don't think you're appreciating."

"Except when he's working on an album," Anise said.

"Yes, but that's like every couple of years," Jada shook her head. "Unfortunately, I married a man who, from day one, had me so low on his to-do list, he didn't even remember that he asked for a reconciliation."

Anise grimaced. "Hush, love."

"I thought it was his first love that came between us, but I completely forgot that I hardly saw my husband while we were married. We had way too many problems to solve." Jada sighed. "We were doomed from the start."

"Funnily enough, that's what Alyssa said about me and Duke."

"Why is she still there?" Jada asked. "I think you would have found some way to get her to leave by now."

"That's what she wants me to do," Anise said. "I can sense her judging me every time she looks at me. I want to prove that I am not the person she assumes I am."

Jada snorted. "Kick her to the curb. She's trouble. Okay, let's go."

Chapter Nineteen

Alyssa paced Nakia's tiny apartment living room. Why had she started the ball rolling on this venture to break up Anise and Duke? They would eventually break up anyway. And what if, by putting Nakia in Duke's path, she created another monstrous relationship? Judging from Nakia's lifestyle, she was probably even worse for Duke than Anise.

Alyssa had overheard her on three different calls in fifteen minutes, lying to three different men about her whereabouts.

Not only was Nakia in high demand, but she also seemed to be involved with them intimately. Maybe Alyssa was too pure for this world because she couldn't fathom juggling multiple men like that—lying so smoothly, so effortlessly. It made her stomach twist.

Alyssa sat down heavily on the worn-out couch, rubbing her temples. What was she even doing? What if her little plan backfired?

She exhaled sharply. "This is a mistake," she muttered under her breath.

"What's a mistake?" Nakia's voice cut through the air as she strolled out of the bedroom, adjusting a pair of large hoop earrings. She was wearing a sheer pantsuit that left nothing to the imagination. She looked radiant and confident—like a woman who had never doubted herself a day in her life.

Alyssa forced a smile. "Just thinking out loud."

Nakia smirked, clearly unconvinced. "Uh-huh. If you're having second thoughts about our little plan, don't. Duke is a grown man. He'll make his own choices."

Alyssa swallowed. "Yeah. He will."

But for the first time, since she had set this whole thing in motion, she wasn't so sure she wanted to see how it would end.

"Do we need to go over this again?" Nakia asked impatiently. "I kind of have a thing tonight. It was already set in stone."

"Are you doing sex work on the side?" Alyssa swallowed. "Because I heard you on the phone with three men."

Nakia laughed. "I have a lot of friends, Alyssa. One of the men who called writes for Loose Lips, the gossip magazine you were wishing you had a contact at. I told him what you told me—I'm on Duke's radar because I resemble Madge, and he wants me to have his baby. He was thinking of going the surrogacy route, but when he saw me, he instantly knew he wanted me to be the mother of his children. And the rumors of his secret relationship with Anise Crystal? Just rumors. She's too unstable to be in a permanent relationship with anyone. How am I doing so far?"

"Uh, great," Alyssa nodded.

"Well then, the only thing left is the pictures," Nakia said. "And tomorrow, we'll have loads of them. I was instantly cast as the lead in the music video as soon as Kenan, the director, saw me dance."

"I really hope Duke likes me as much as you say," she continued, "because I could really use a break right now. A rich music superstar is just what the doctor ordered for my ailing bank account."

She cackled while applying her contacts, then batted her overly long fake eyelashes at Alyssa. "For this date, I have green eyes. Don't ask."

Alyssa sighed. "Trust me, I won't."

****

The music video set was, as usual, buzzing with activity. Duke had a low, thrumming headache—too many late nights and early mornings, and his brain was fried. He sat in a quiet corner of the set, nursing a bottle of water, hoping for a few minutes of peace before they called him back to perform.

Just then, Nakia slid into the seat next to him, her perfume a soft, intoxicating scent that seemed to cling to the air. She was dressed in a figure-hugging black dress that accentuated every curve, her long hair cascading in waves down her back. She gave him a smile that was more playful than innocent.

"Rough day?" she asked, her voice sultry like she knew exactly what kind of trouble she could cause.

Duke looked up at her, giving a tired smile. "Just the usual. Long shoot, early call times." He ran a hand through his hair, trying to shake off the fatigue. "But you look like you're having a good time."

"Oh, I am," Nakia purred, her gaze lingering on him as she leaned in slightly. "But I've been meaning to ask you...

how do you keep up with everything? You're always so... calm under pressure."

Duke chuckled dryly, feeling the weight of the day pressing down on him. "Experience, I guess," he said, his voice a little more clipped than he intended.

Nakia didn't seem to notice—or maybe she didn't care. She shifted closer, her hand brushing his arm lightly as she spoke again, her tone laced with unmistakable flirtation. "I bet it's not just experience. You must have a secret—some way of handling all the chaos. Maybe you can share it with me sometime?"

Her fingers lingered on his arm for just a moment too long before pulling away. Her eyes locked on his, dark and steady, her smile suggesting there was more beneath the surface than she was letting on.

He knew her type. He dealt with women like this every day. They didn't see him as a person; they saw him as a purse.

He leaned back in his chair, trying to ignore the corny thoughts ricocheting through his head. He was indeed tired. "I don't know about secrets. Just trying to get through the day without losing my mind."

Nakia tilted her head, her lips curving into a teasing smile. "Well, maybe you could lose your mind with me for a bit. You know, take a break from all the responsibility and just enjoy yourself. I'm very good at helping people relax."

Her words hung in the air between them. Duke grimaced in revulsion and looked away, focusing on the hum of the crew around them. How can I let her down easy? He wasn't interested or even remotely attracted to her.

"I am in a committed relationship with a girlfriend who I love and am faithful to, so I won't be taking you up on that offer..." His voice trailed off.

Nakia didn't seem disappointed, though. Instead, she gave

him another lingering look, as if she could already picture what it would be like if he did give in.

"I'll be around," she said softly, her tone a little too suggestive. "Whenever you're ready, Duke."

Chapter Nineteen

Anise stretched, the soft linen of the guest bed clinging to her as she slowly came to full consciousness. She blinked in confusion for a moment, disoriented by the unfamiliar surroundings. The soft sunlight filtering in through the curtains reminded her where she was—Jada's guest room. She smiled to herself, today was a big day. She was going to tell her children and Grandma Saidie about Duke. The thought brought a nervous excitement that fluttered in her chest.

She reached for her phone, hoping to find a message or a missed call from Duke. But as she unlocked the screen, she saw that every call she had made to him the night before had gone unanswered. A small wave of unease washed over her, but she pushed it aside. Duke had been busy with work, she reminded herself. He would call when he could.

Still, she couldn't deny the twinge of disappointment.

She'd hoped for him to meet Grandma Saidie after the expo, to introduce him to the family. It was an important step, and she wanted it to happen. She made a mental note to try calling him again later.

Rolling out of bed, Anise padded to the window and peeked outside. The sun was rising, casting a warm glow over the back garden. She sighed contentedly. There was something about the quiet of the morning before everything got hectic that made her feel at peace.

She wondered how her children and Grandma Saidie would handle her introducing a man she was in a relationship with. Cinnamon would be nonchalant—after all, she was the one who had suggested she talk to him in the first place. Cayenne would be unsurprised—she heard all the news before everyone else at the hairdressing parlor where she worked. And Sage would be excited and supportive. Of the three girls, Sage was the most invested in her finally finding love and happiness.

Grandma Saidie would be cordial and sweet, but if she had even the faintest whiff of doubt about Duke's motives or intentions, she would pull her aside and say, Anise, that man is trouble.

She made her way to the bathroom, got in the shower, and began preparing for the day ahead.

When she got out of the shower, she tried Duke's phone again.

He answered after the third ring.

"Hey, Anise."

"Duke, what's going on?" she asked. "I got no responses to my calls last night."

"So sorry," Duke groaned. "I had a massive headache. Haven't had one like this in a while. After we wrapped up shooting the video, I took some tablets that Chex gave me, and they knocked me out. I mean totally."

"Oh," Anise said, concerned. "How are you feeling now?"

"Good, I guess," Duke muttered. "Still a little sleepy. I wonder what kind of tablets those were. How's it going on your end?"

"Today is the expo. I was wondering if you wanted to drop by."

"And see you in a wedding dress?" Duke chuckled. "Of course."

Anise smiled.

"I should just take a wedding officiant with me and call it an event."

"Don't tempt me," Anise teased, running a hand through her damp curls. "I might just say yes."

Duke laughed, but there was something a little off in his tone. Anise's smile faded slightly. Maybe he was still groggy from whatever Chex had given him.

"You sure you're okay?" she asked again.

"Yeah, yeah. I'll be fine," Duke assured her. "I just need to shake this off."

Anise hesitated. "If you're not up to it, you don't have to push yourself to come today."

"Nah, I want to be there—if even briefly," he said. "I want to see you in a bridal gown. I have a retake at the studio at twelve, so I can't stay."

"Okay. I'll see you later, then."

"See you later," Duke echoed, his voice softer now.

Anise ended the call and sat on the edge of the bed for a moment, pressing the phone against her lips. Something still nagged at her, but she brushed it aside.

Today was a big day. Duke would be there, and soon, her family would finally meet him.

And she wanted everything to go perfectly.

Jada was up and about when Anise stepped out. She was already dressed.

"Morning, lovely lady." She blew Anise a kiss. "That's exactly how I want you to wear your hair with the dress."

Anise looked in the mirror. "This is just a basic curly updo that I did to take my hair out of the way."

"Love it. It's perfect," Jada said. "Your girls are all doing their hair and makeup the way it was on their wedding day, and they're fixing up Grandma Saidie. They're so excited about it."

Anise chuckled. "Duke said he'll be stopping by. I intend to officially introduce him to everyone."

"Great!" Jada nodded. "It's about time."

"Do you think I should do it so publicly, though?" Anise asked. "Or should I ask him to meet me at their hotel after?"

"Or before," Jada said. "I'm going to deliver Grandma Saidie's dress, and I want all my living mannequins to get ready together—that includes you, Miss."

"He can meet you at the hotel. You make a quick introduction, chit-chat a little, and then get ready with the others. It'll be perfect—you won't have to wait around to introduce him, you'll get it out of the way, and you'll be in a more casual environment with just them."

"Great idea," Anise said. "Let me call him."

****

Duke arrived at the Dorchester, a pretty boutique hotel on the hip strip. He didn't know why he was feeling nervous. He already knew Anise's daughters. It was the significance of the moment that was making him feel this way. When Anise called him and said she was finally ready to introduce him to her family, his heart somersaulted. This was it! This was the moment that proved they were really serious.

He looked in the car mirror: clean-shaven, level brows, the usual handsome face stared back at him. He took a deep breath. After chatting in the penthouse lounge a couple of weeks ago, Cinnamon, Cayenne, and Sage were already fine with him. His only worry was Grandma Saidie.

What if she didn't like him? She was Anise's relationship filter. He was aware of her role in Anise's life as the voice of reason, the one who could see a person's character.

He exhaled slowly, gripping the steering wheel for a second before stepping out of the car. The morning sun bathed the Dorchester in a warm glow, and he could hear the rhythmic sounds of the waves crashing nearby. It was going to be a beautiful day.

Duke adjusted his blazer, squared his shoulders, and headed inside. They were to meet at the restaurant on the terrace for breakfast.

He spotted them immediately—Anise, radiant as always, her daughters chatting animatedly, and beside them, a petite woman with sharp eyes and a knowing expression. Grandma Saidie.

Anise looked up first, her face lighting up as she saw him. She stood, smoothing her dress, and gestured him over. "There you are," she said warmly.

He leaned in and kissed her cheek. "Didn't keep you waiting too long, did I?"

"No, perfect timing," she assured him before turning to the older woman. "Grandma, this is Duke."

Grandma Saidie's eyes swept over him, measuring, weighing. Duke extended his hand, and after a moment's pause, she took it.

"Duke, hmm?" she mused, her grip surprisingly firm for her small frame. "I like your song, 'No Promises.'"

"You do?" Duke raised an eyebrow. "I would have pegged you as a person who liked 'It's Always You.'"

"'It's Always You' is too sappy," Saidie said irreverently. "'No Promises' is edgier."

Cinnamon snickered behind her glass of orange juice. "Didn't Mom tell you our granny isn't the standard type?"

"She still goes to Dover to watch the car races," Cayenne said.

"And she has a boyfriend," Sage chuckled. "We heard all about him while we were coming here. Maybe that's why she doesn't want any promises."

Duke laughed.

Grandma Saidie gave a mock-stern look, shaking her head. "You girls are too fast with your mouths." But the sparkle in her eyes told Duke she was enjoying this.

"I like a woman who knows what she wants," Duke said, settling into his seat. "And I respect anyone who still enjoys a good car race."

Grandma Saidie took a sip of her tea. "Well, if you're serious about Anise, you should know—she comes from a line of women who don't waste time on foolishness."

Anise sighed. "Grandma…"

"What? He should know." She turned back to Duke, her sharp gaze assessing him once more. "So tell me, young man, why should I believe you're not here to waste her time?"

The table went quiet, all eyes shifting to Duke.

Duke met Grandma Saidie's gaze steadily. "Because I know what I have in Anise," he said, his voice sure. "And I'd be a fool to waste it."

A slow smile spread across Saidie's face. "Hmph." She took another sip of tea, then nodded. "That's a good start."

Cinnamon clapped lightly. "Congratulations, Duke. You made it past level one."

Duke chuckled. "How many levels are there?"

Grandma Saidie set down her cup. "That depends. We'll see how you do with breakfast."

Laughter rippled through the table, and Anise squeezed Duke's hand under the table. He exhaled, the tension easing from his shoulders.

This was good stuff. Family and togetherness. He was feeling genuinely happy.

Chapter Twenty

The expo was buzzing with excitement, the large convention hall filled with a vibrant mix of fashion enthusiasts, bridal designers, photographers, and wedding planners. Stalls were decorated in pastel tones, and the air was thick with the scent of fresh flowers and the hum of chatter. The sound of heels clicking on the polished floor echoed as people drifted from booth to booth, admiring the latest trends in wedding attire and décor. Soft music played in the background, adding to the lively yet refined atmosphere.

Jada's booth was a beacon of creativity, the space filled with elegant displays of her wedding dress designs. The centerpiece was a stunning display featuring a delicate lace gown with intricate beading that caught the light perfectly. Guests paused to admire the dresses, and the buzz around her designs grew as the day went on. Her reputation for impeccable taste had preceded her, and today, it was evident in the glowing admiration she received from those who passed by.

Duke had stopped by briefly, adding to the buzz around her booth. He admired Anise in her dress, kissed her quickly, and left.

Anise stood with her daughters and Grandma Saidie, chatting and laughing together casually. They twisted and turned whenever someone pointed at one of their dresses. It was a fun moment.

"We should do this more often," Anise said to the group.

"We definitely should," Cinnamon nodded, "before you get bogged down with marriage and children again."

Anise laughed. "I had one introduction, and you are already hearing wedding bells."

"What are you waiting on?" Grandma Saidie asked. "He is besotted with you. You can see it rolling off him. I like Duke Jones; he is a rare, decent man."

"So that's your stamp of approval?" Anise asked.

"That's it," Saidie nodded. "He is a keeper."

Anise smiled.

Just as Anise was about to respond, a young woman approached the booth, her eyes wide with excitement.

"Excuse me," she said, glancing between them. "Are you Anise Crystal?"

Anise turned. "Yes, I am."

The woman let out a small squeal. "I knew it! You are my personal hero. I was telling my friend that it was you. I have watched all your interviews, and I must tell you that speaking up about abuse makes a difference."

"Aw, thank you," Anise said, hugging her.

"It's because of you I had the courage to seek help and start having healthier relationships. I'm getting married in six months."

Anise's heart swelled as she pulled the young woman into a gentle hug. "I'm so glad to hear that. It means everything to know that sharing my story has helped you."

The woman wiped her eyes, her voice trembling with emotion. "You gave me the strength to leave an unhealthy relationship. And now, I'm getting married to someone who truly loves me for who I am. You've changed my life."

Anise's eyes softened as she pulled back, taking the woman's hands in hers. "You did all the hard work. You chose yourself, and that's the most important step. I'm so proud of you."

The woman nodded, wiping her eyes again. "Thank you so much. I'll be thinking of you when I walk down the aisle."

Anise felt a warmth in her chest as the woman left, waving goodbye with a grateful smile. Her daughters and Grandma Saidie stood silently for a moment, taking in the exchange.

"That's why I admire you so much, Anise," Grandma Saidie said, her voice thick with pride. "You were not afraid to speak up and speak out. Doing that helps."

Anise laughed softly, wiping her eyes and feeling unexpectedly emotional. "I just want to make a difference. Even if it's in small ways."

Sage, always the thoughtful one, grinned. "You're definitely making waves, Mom. No small ways about it."

Anise chuckled. "Well, I'll just keep riding the wave then."

Cinnamon raised an eyebrow. "Speaking of riding waves... when is Duke going to make things official? We all see it."

Anise shot her daughter a playful look. "You are relentless."

Grandma Saidie smirked. "She's right, though. You know what you've got. Don't let him get away."

Anise rolled her eyes, but her smile couldn't hide the warmth spreading through her. "Let's just enjoy the moment, okay? I've got plenty of time to think about all that."

"But don't wait too long," Grandma Saidie teased, winking. "You are not getting any younger."

Anise laughed, her heart full. It was moments like this, filled with laughter, love, and connection, that made everything she had built so worth it.

The day went smoothly. Jada was inundated with customers; her booth was by far the most popular of them all, so it was no surprise when the announcement came that the winner of the coveted Bridal Magazine cover had been decided. The room grew still. Anise gave Jada a thumbs-up. Jada looked as nervous as ever.

All eyes were on the stage, waiting for the verdict. The air seemed to crackle with anticipation. The editor-in-chief of the magazine took the mic and smiled warmly as she announced Jada's name. "And this month's Bridal Magazine cover will go to the brilliant Jada Tinsdale!"

The crowd erupted in applause, and Jada beamed, her eyes sparkling with surprise and gratitude. She had worked so hard to get to this point, and now, it was paying off. Anise rushed forward to congratulate her, hugging her tight as Jada laughed with excitement.

After the announcement, the booth slowly emptied as the expo wound down. The energy of the day had been electric, but now the hall was quieting down. Cinnamon, Cayenne, Sage, and Grandma Saidie left to go back to their hotel.

Anise went with them to hang out for a while and then returned to help Jada pack up.

"This is the not-so-fun part," Jada said tiredly when Anise returned. "We should have hired help."

"I know what you mean," Tarique walked over. "Congrats on the Bridal Magazine win."

"Thanks," Jada smirked.

"I see you borrowed my idea to have an older woman in a

wedding dress and went one step further to hire a celebrity to attract a crowd to your booth," Tarique glared at Anise.

Anise chuckled. "I wasn't hired; I did it for free. Jada and I have been friends forever."

Tarique shrugged. "Next year, I'm hiring models and a celebrity too."

"I said I wasn't hired," Anise growled.

"Well, your presence did cause a stir," Tarique said, "no doubt in part because of the article in Loose Lips magazine."

"Who reads that trash?" Anise said. "My life has been so boring lately, I doubt anything they write is true."

Tarique whipped out the magazine from his back pocket and sat down in one of the plastic chairs.

The headline was: Duke's New Love: Madge 2.0? Beneath the headline was a picture of Duke, his lips pressed close to a woman's ear. The woman was Nakia.

"What on earth?" Anise muttered. "Let me see that."

Tarique handed her the paper.

She read aloud: DJ Duke, our beloved artiste, may be on the road to finding love again. Forget the speculation about his secret love being Anise Crystal; he is well and truly smitten with Nakia Sanders, our friendly local realtor at Lansdown Realtors.

Nakia said their connection was love at first sight. The popular DJ asked her to star in his latest video, "Tried and True," a catchy tune in collaboration with DJ Salky. And their charismatic session has led to a torrid night of passion, which Nakia said they both won't soon forget. Sources close to the couple have confirmed that the pair have been inseparable ever since. But the real bombshell came when Nakia revealed to Loose Lips that Duke had made a monumental request—he asked her to be the mother of his children. He was going to use a surrogate, but now that he has found her, he will not anymore.

"Duke is everything I've ever wanted in a man," Nakia was quoted saying, her eyes glowing with excitement. "He's kind, successful, and knows exactly what he wants. When he asked me to be the mother of his children, I was speechless. I couldn't say yes fast enough. We're already planning for the future."

The revelation has set tongues wagging, leaving many wondering what this means for Duke's past relationships, particularly with Anise Crystal, who has long been a fan favorite to land in his arms. Sources close to Anise remain tight-lipped about the matter, but some speculate that the strong bond between the two may have been tested in recent months.

Jada chuckled. "Who writes these things? It's ridiculous."

Anise shook her head. "Is it, though?"

"Of course it is," Jada nudged her. "Give Tarique back his paper, and let's go."

Anise handed Tarique the paper and smiled. "Well, that certainly was entertaining."

Tarique nodded. "I thought so. Anyway, kiddos, see you next year."

Jada nodded.

Anise turned to her. "How did Loose Lips know that Duke wants children?"

"An assumption," Jada said. "But we all know Duke wouldn't ask a random woman to have his children. It's made up."

"What if it's not?" Anise hissed. "I couldn't reach him last night. His excuse was that he had a headache. I don't know of Duke having headaches, and it's the first time in our entire relationship that I called him and didn't get him. He always responds! He never ignores me."

Jada sighed.

"I can't believe he cheated on me."

"Now, Anise," Jada said, "don't get carried away."

"He is like every typical Jamaican man—randy dogs."

"Good Lord," Jada whistled. "Anise, please."

"I'm going to bounce," Anise said. "I may be sleeping over at your place tonight."

Jada sighed. "Okay. See you at home."

Chapter Twenty-One

Anise's heart raced as she walked out of the expo hall, the chaos of the day seeming like a distant memory. Her mind was consumed by the revelation in Loose Lips, the article she couldn't shake from her thoughts. Her body felt like it was moving on autopilot as she left the venue, heading straight to her car. She couldn't believe it—Duke had asked Nakia to be the mother of his children? The words seemed like a bad joke, but the pain in her chest was all too real.

She slid into the driver's seat and pulled her phone from her purse. She dialed his number and waited, each ring making her feel more and more frantic. Finally, he picked up.

"Anise?" Duke's voice sounded sleepy.

"Where are you?" Anise asked.

"At home," Duke said. "I did the retakes and decided to take a break."

"What's up, are you coming home now?"

"Yes," Anise hissed. "But only to pack!"

"Why do you sound like that?" Duke asked, perturbed.

"Because I just read an article about you and Nakia in a gossip rag called Loose Lips."

"So?" Duke asked.

"So!" Anise screeched. "You were having a grand romance with her all this time. That's what's up."

"That's crazy talk," Duke said.

"Then why does she know specific and private information about you? Like the fact that you were going to use a surrogate?" Anise asked. "And to think I introduced you to my family! And I was about to ditch my birth control and tell you we should try for a baby! I feel humiliated. And why did you have your lips on her ear?"

"It was just a scene from the music video. A gazillion people were there. After we finished the scene, I didn't even see her leave. I went to bed with a headache."

"It's over!" Anise said.

"Just like that?" Duke sounded defeated. "You're just going to play judge, jury, and executioner on our relationship because of a silly article?"

The way he said it made Anise pause. "How would she know about you wanting to go the surrogate route?"

"Alyssa," Duke said. "This has Alyssa written all over it. She said she would test us. I have no doubt she sent her vampish friend to try to seduce me yesterday. I didn't take the bait. And now you read an article and are ready to ditch me? Weren't you the one who said that these gossip magazines are full of crap?"

"I, uh…" Anise inhaled and then sighed. "Cheating is a trigger."

"I know," Duke said. "You told me, and I told you that

I don't cheat. It's not my style. I've never cheated in a relationship, and I never will."

"Nakia does have a passing resemblance to Madge," Anise said. "Madge is your first love."

"Are you coming home so we can have this conversation face to face?" Duke asked.

Anise sighed. "Yes. Don't say anything to Alyssa, will you? I don't want her to know that her little stunt had an impact."

Duke chuckled. "I won't."

Anise hung up, her fingers still clenched around her phone. Her heart was still hammering, but the sharp edge of betrayal had dulled into something more complicated—uncertainty, frustration, and the nagging awareness that she might have jumped to conclusions too quickly.

She tossed her phone onto the passenger seat and gripped the steering wheel, staring at the streetlights flickering against the darkened sky. Alyssa. So this was what Alyssa had been hinting at? And she almost took the bait.

Duke sounded so sure. So calm. So him.

Anise exhaled and started the car. She wasn't ready to let this go yet, but maybe she owed him the chance to say it to her face.

By the time she pulled into the driveway, her nerves had settled into a slow burn rather than a full blaze. She grabbed her purse, squared her shoulders, and stepped out.

The front door swung open before she even reached it, and there was Duke, standing barefoot in sweats and a T-shirt, his hair slightly messy like he'd run his fingers through it too many times. His expression was wary, but there was something else there too—relief.

Anise crossed her arms. "Talk."

Duke didn't hesitate. "I love you. Not Nakia, not anyone

else. And if Alyssa thought she could shake that, she underestimated me—and us."

Anise searched his face, looking for cracks, for signs of deception, for anything that might confirm her worst fears. But there was only sincerity.

"I almost left," she admitted, her voice softer now.

"But you didn't," Duke said.

She swallowed, feeling the weight of everything that had almost slipped away. "No. I didn't."

Duke stepped forward, closing the distance between them. "So what does this mean, Anise? Have we grown? Have we passed the test?"

"I don't know about tests," Anise looked at him thoughtfully. "But I do know that I love and trust you, and I can't believe I am saying this, but I am ready for all of it—the good, the bad, and the indifferent. Once we are chugging along together, I'll take whatever comes our way."

Duke cupped her face. "Do you know how long I've waited to hear this?"

"Three years," Anise smiled.

"About that," Duke kissed her, a kiss full of tenderness and promise as if trying to convey everything that words couldn't quite capture. When they broke apart, he rested his forehead against hers, his voice low and sincere.

"I've never been more sure of anything, Anise. I've been waiting for this moment—for you to truly trust me and be ready for all of it."

She closed her eyes, letting the warmth of his words settle deep in her chest. It was a relief, a release, to finally let go of the doubt, the fear, and the uncertainty that had clouded her mind for so long.

"I'm ready, Duke," she whispered, her voice steady but soft. "I've been scared, but now I know we can handle anything together."

Duke stepped back just enough to look at her thoroughly, his eyes still holding that mixture of affection and awe. "Then let's stop wasting time," he said, his grin returning, playful now. "Let's make the most of what we've got. And make it ours."

Anise couldn't help but smile in return. The weight of everything they'd been through was still there, but it was no longer an obstacle. It was a part of their story that had led them here—together, stronger than before.

"Absolutely," she said, her heart lighter than it had been in weeks. "Let's do this."

And with that, Duke pulled her back into his arms, holding her close as if he never intended to let her go again.

Chapter Twenty-Two

The morning after, Anise was downstairs, skimming through the copy of Loose Lips that she was sure Alyssa had left out on the nook for her to find. Duke was still taking a shower. They were going to spend the day together—ring shopping and planning their simple wedding.

"Oh, what a beautiful morning," Alyssa said loudly. She paused when she saw Anise. "You are still here?"

"Yup," Anise said.

"And you are reading the article?"

"Oh yes," Anise nodded. "Interesting read."

"And you are not mad?" Alyssa sat across from her.

"I was initially," Anise said. "I was livid, and then I called Duke, and he said he would never hurt me that way. I calmed down, came home, told him I loved him, agreed to marry him, and try for a baby."

"Oh," Alyssa sighed in relief. "Thank God for that."

Anise looked at her curiously. "What's the matter? I thought you planned all of this to break us up, to prove how abnormal I was."

"No," Alyssa shook her head. "I planned it to test you both. Nakia looked like Madge. I was wondering if Duke would take the bait, and you supposedly had a short fuse, so I thought you would cut him off like you do all of your other relationships."

"Duke is not like anyone else I've ever dated," Anise said. "He's different," Anise continued, her voice soft but firm. "He's the one person I don't want to lose. I know I can be hot-headed sometimes, but with him, I want to do better. I want to make this work."

Alyssa studied her for a moment, then smiled, her eyes softening. "I can see that," she said quietly. "And trust me when I tell you this: I am genuinely happy to hear that. When I was in cahoots with Nakia, I was worried for a moment. Suddenly, I thought, 'But Anise is not bad for Duke. What am I doing? What if he falls for Nakia, now that would be a mistake times a hundred.'"

Anise laughed.

"Trust me," Alyssa said, "I was worried yesterday, and then Nakia called me in the night crying and said, 'Duke said he is not interested in me. He has a girlfriend, and he is faithful.' And then I thought, 'Duke passed with flying colors. Now it's Anise's turn.' And look at that, you trust each other."

Alyssa leaned back in her chair, folding her arms, looking thoughtful. "Well, I guess I've got to hand it to you both. You proved me wrong. I won't refuse a wedding invitation this time if you two are going to make it official."

Anise chuckled, folding the magazine closed and setting it down. "Small wedding in a few days. We decided to just go for it."

"Well, congrats," Alyssa nodded. "I wish for you both all the happiness in the world."

Just then, Duke emerged from the hallway, freshly showered. He stopped when he saw Alyssa. "Everything okay in here?" he asked, his tone concerned.

Anise looked up at him, her heart swelling. "Yeah," she said softly. "Everything's fine."

Alyssa stood up, giving him a pleased look. "I am proud of you for resisting Nakia. And I am glad to see that you and Anise really have something special."

Duke raised an eyebrow. "Why Nakia, though?"

"I theorized that you have a type," Alyssa said apologetically. "I didn't account for the fact that you might be different with Anise. I thought you might go for someone more like Nakia, but you proved me wrong. And I'm glad for that. I can see the way you look at her—this is real."

Duke smiled, his gaze softening as he looked at Anise. "Yeah, it's real. More than I ever thought it could be."

Anise's heart fluttered at his words. It was moments like these, when the world seemed to fall away, that she knew they were making the right decision.

Alyssa gave them both a nod, a faint smile on her lips. "Well, I guess I can't keep holding out on you two. Go, get on with your plans. Just make sure to invite me to the wedding, alright?"

"We will," Anise promised. "It's happening soon, but we'll make sure you're there."

Alyssa's eyes sparkled. "Good, I'll be there. Can't wait to see you both officially make it."

As Alyssa left, Anise turned to Duke, her expression one of love and contentment. "Well, that was... unexpected. When I first met her, she rubbed me the wrong way."

"Alyssa was just being Alyssa," Duke chuckled and

walked over to her, pulling her close. "Yeah, but I think it worked out. I'm proud of us."

Anise smiled, pressing a kiss to his chest. "I'm proud of us, too."

They stood there for a moment, just holding each other, the weight of everything settling around them. Then Duke gently pulled away, his hand slipping into hers. "So, about that ring shopping? You ready?"

Anise laughed, feeling lighter than ever. "Let's go. I'm ready for the rest of our lives."

Hand in hand, they walked out together; the future stretched before them like an open road. They were ready for whatever came next—together.

****

"Today on Claire Talk, we are about to discuss being "Tried and True." DJ Duke wrote the hottest song on the airwaves for his longtime love, Anise Crystal, and we need to dig deep into that as a concept.

"By the way, congratulations to Anise Crystal and DJ Duke! They eloped in a private wedding at their house. I was invited but sworn to secrecy until they left on their super-secret honeymoon. The wedding was perfect, and everything screamed "just for them." It was small, intimate, and full of love—exactly how they wanted it. There were no big crowds, no media frenzy, just them and the people they care about most. It was everything a couple like Anise and Duke deserved after all the ups and downs they've faced in their pasts and together.

"Now, back to the song "Tried and True." Let me tell you, if you haven't heard it yet—it's a masterpiece. DJ Duke has always been known for his smooth sound, but this track? It hits different. He's not just singing about love; he's living it. His lyrics are raw, honest, and vulnerable in a way we rarely see from him. He wrote this song for Anise; you can feel every ounce of that love in every word.

"But here's where it gets interesting—"Tried and True" isn't just a love song. It's a testament to resilience. It's about going through the fire and coming out stronger, standing by each other when the world wants to tear you apart. It's about loyalty, commitment, and trust—the cornerstones of any solid relationship. And DJ Duke? He's got all of that with Anise.

"They've been through so much, yet here they are, stronger than ever, proving that love isn't just about the good times but about how you weather the storms together. It's rare to see a couple who are so unapologetically themselves, who have faced challenges but keep rising above them. That's what makes their bond so unique, and that's exactly what DJ Duke captured in "Tried and True."

"So, today on Claire Talk, we're diving deep into what it really means to be "tried and true" in love. How do we apply this concept to our own relationships? What does it take to make love last, through thick and thin? Let's talk about that and much more as we celebrate Anise and Duke's love and beautiful journey together.

"Stick with me, folks. This is going to be a conversation you don't want to miss."

The End

Excerpt Stay With Me (Book 5 Ridgeview Series)

It was pouring outside. Jada was happy that she'd had the good sense not to try to drive back to Kingston. Her only regret was that she hadn't taken any food from the wedding reception with her.

Anise and Duke had laid out a spread at their wedding. She wished she had eaten more, but between her duties as matron of honor and catching up with old friends, she had barely managed more than a few bites.

Now, sitting in the cozy guest cottage at her estranged husband's house, she could feel the hunger creeping in.

She should have planned her overnight stay better. She should have at least brought snacks—or better yet, booked a hotel. But that would have been an unjustified, unnecessary expense when Richard had begged her to stay here so they could work things out with their marriage.

Unfortunately, he had left six weeks ago for the Bahamas to work on a project he was involved with over there. And she had gone back to Kingston, only returning sporadically to help her best friend Anise plan her wedding.

It had been small, intimate, and private, with just their families and a few close friends attending. Jada had slept over at Anise's place last night because Anise had planned a pajama bachelorette party, where her girls, her grandmother Saidie, and a couple of girlfriends had camped out in the living room, drinking wine, playing games, and reminiscing about old times.

It had been a night filled with laughter—something Jada had needed more than she realized. But now, with the wedding over and the festivities behind her, she was alone again.

The rain wasn't letting up, and the rhythmic drumming against the roof made the silence inside feel heavier. Her stomach growled again. She got up and checked the refrigerator. It was filled with bottled water—and nothing else.

She was seriously contemplating pulling on some clothes and trudging next door to Anise's house to raid her fridge. That's how desperate she was. She would interrupt her friend's first night with Duke as husband and wife just to eat.

They were leaving for Bali for their honeymoon first thing tomorrow anyway. All that yummy food would be going to waste.

She looked down at her shorts and T-shirt. She'd be soaked by the time she got back, and this was the only nightwear she had packed. She didn't even have a raincoat. And what if Anise and Duke didn't answer their door? The rain was coming down in sheets—it would take someone with bionic hearing to catch her paltry knocks on their heavy front door. And by then she would be soaked and still hungry.

She glanced at her phone. Still no service. This was shaping up to be the longest night on record. It was ten o'clock, according to her phone. She checked the cupboards again but didn't find any food.

Tomorrow, she would stock the place to the brim with all the nonperishable items she could find so that if by some chance she came back here, at least she'd have something to eat.

For now, she would slowly sip a bottle of water and daydream about all the delicious food at the reception she hadn't gotten to enjoy.

Anise had wanted a total Jamaican experience. There was curried goat, oxtail, escoveitch fish, jerk chicken, bammy, rice and peas, festival, and plantain—not to mention the salads. She should have had a salad. And she could have at least taken something from the overladen dessert table.

The fruit cake had looked so good, and the sweet potato pudding had been served with ice cream.

Jada groaned and flopped back onto the couch. Her mouth watered just thinking about it.

She took a sip of water and sighed. Maybe she could just go to sleep and ignore her hunger.

But even as she closed her eyes, her stomach let out another loud, embarrassing growl, mocking her attempts at self-control.

And then—just as she was debating whether pride or hunger would win—a knock sounded at the door.

Jada sat up fast, heart pounding. Who in their right mind would be out in this weather? Maybe it was just the wind driving something against the door. But then the knock sounded again, louder this time.

She hesitated for a second before swinging her legs off the couch and padding cautiously toward the door. She cracked it open just enough to see who it was—and her breath hitched.

Richard.

Drenched from head to toe, rain dripping from his hair, his shirt plastered to his body. He looked gorgeous, his chiseled face partly shadowed by the dim porch light, but she could still make out the sharp angles of his jawline and the determined set of his mouth. His dark eyes, always intense, locked onto hers with an unreadable expression—a mixture of exhaustion, relief, and something deeper. Something that made her pulse quicken despite herself.

His thick brows were furrowed slightly, droplets of water clinging to his lashes, making him look both rugged and impossibly handsome. His full lips, slightly parted as if he was about to speak, sent a rush of memories crashing into her. How many times had she kissed those lips? How many times had she run her fingers through that rain-darkened hair?

His broad shoulders rose and fell with steady breaths, the soaked fabric of his shirt clinging to every defined muscle, highlighting the strength she used to take for granted. His skin, a deep, warm brown, gleamed under the sheen of rain, making him look like he had just walked off the cover of a romance novel.

Jada swallowed hard.

Richard stood there, raking his curls from his brow. "Hello, wife. Are you going to let me in?"

"Nope," Jada said breathlessly.

"Come on, Jay," he said huskily. "I have enough takeout for four people, and the bag with my clothes is getting wet."

"Takeout?" She opened the door wider.

Richard smiled and held up a bag with a popular fast-food label on it. "I was ravenously hungry when I left the airport. I was hoping you'd break bread with me—and maybe put me up for the night."

Jada licked her lips. "Come on in. I don't know how you sensed it, but I was hungry as hell." She took the food from him.

"I'll just have a quick shower," he said. "It's crazy out there. And to think I almost didn't venture so far out here—but I heard you were staying here, and I didn't want you leaving tomorrow without seeing you face to face... to plead my case. You look good, by the way."

Jada ignored the warmth creeping up her neck at his compliment and focused on unpacking the food. She didn't need Richard sweet-talking her—not when she was starving and vulnerable to both good food and familiar chemistry.

"I'm sure you rehearsed that on the way over," she

muttered, pulling out a box of fries and popping one into her mouth.

Richard chuckled, already moving toward the bathroom. "I didn't have to. It's the truth."

Jada rolled her eyes, but his deep, husky voice lingered in the air like a whisper against her skin. She heard the bathroom door click shut, followed by the rush of water, and she exhaled heavily.

This was a bad idea, a very bad idea.

Richard had a way of getting under her skin, slipping past her defenses with a look, a touch, a well-placed word. She told herself she was only letting him stay because of the storm, because it would be cruel to send him back out in this weather.

But she knew better.

Fifteen minutes later, Richard reemerged, dressed in a plain white T-shirt and sweatpants, his damp curls messier than before. He looked so effortlessly good that it was infuriating. He glanced at the spread she had laid out on the small table and grinned.

"I really did go overboard with the ordering, didn't I?"

"You did," Jada said, biting into her sandwich. "But I'm so grateful."

Richard sat across from her, watching her for a moment before picking up his meal. "I missed this," he admitted, his voice quieter now.

Jada swallowed and met his gaze. "What? Fast food?"

He shook his head, his expression softening. "Sitting with you. Talking. Just… being here."

She forced a laugh, trying to ignore the pull in her chest. "I wouldn't have guessed that, with the two-year distance between us and all."

Richard's jaw tightened. "We both needed space. We didn't

handle losing our baby well. If we hadn't had that cooling-off period, we may have never recovered."

"Right," she muttered. "Losing the baby was one thing. But we weren't compatible in the least, which is why I have no idea why you want us to have a trial period. And then, when I actually showed up for the requested trial period, you left for the Bahamas. You give me too many mixed signals. The truth is—you're too busy to be a husband."

"I'm partnering with an old friend to create a place just like Ridgeview in the Bahamas," he said. "He ran into some structural problems. It was an emergency that took us weeks to sort out. It was ill-timed and unavoidable—but trust me when I say this, Jada: I want to be your husband again. I want us to try again. This time will be different."

Jada snorted. "I'm not sure about that."

Discover Exclusive Offers and Be the First to Know!

If you haven't already, don't miss out on the opportunity to join my New Release Newsletter! Sign up today and become part of an exclusive community where you'll be among the first to hear about my latest book releases and take advantage of special prices.

Why join my mailing list?

Be the First: Get a head start and be the first to know when I release a new book.

Exclusive Discounts: Unlock special prices available only to subscribers. Enjoy limited time offers and save big on your favorite books.

Quick and Easy: Signing up takes less than 30 seconds.

To join, visit https://www.brenalbar.com/newsletter or scan the QR code below.

Thank you for your support, and happy reading!

Ridgeview Series

The Ridgeview series follows five couples on the Jamaican north coast in the luxurious community of Ridgeview. It explores their everyday struggles with careers, children, and family drama. Each book touches on love, marriage, and trust as the characters face challenges that test their relationships.

Ride or Die (Book 1)
Play For Keeps (Book 2)
Through Thick and Thin (Book 3)
Tried and True (Book 4)
Stay With You (Book 5)

Spice and Stone Series

Join three extraordinary girls—Cinnamon, Cayenne, and Sage—as they navigate the intricate flavors of life, love, and romance in the captivating Spice and Stone series.

Cinnamon (Book 1)
Cayenne (Book 2)
Sage (Book3)

The Crimson Hill Series

Where family drama, romance, and a touch of sci-fi blend seamlessly in the enchanting backdrop of a small town in Jamaica. Prepare to embark on an unforgettable journey as secrets unravel, passions ignite, and destinies intertwine.

No Goodbye (Book 1)
No Misunderstanding (Book 2)
No Ordinary Love (Book 3)
No Fairy Tale (Book 4)
No Letting Go (Book 5)
No Strings Attached (Book 6)
No More Mrs. Nice Girl (Book 7)
No Place Like You (Book 8)
Knight and Day (Book 8.5)
No Expectations (Book 9)
Ice and Fyre (Book 9.5)
No Surrender (Book 10)
No Time for Love (Book 11)
No Promises (Book 12)
Winter's Eve (Book 13)

The Wiley Brothers

Step into the world of the Wiley Brothers, where tragedy weaves an unbreakable bond and love becomes their guiding light. In this captivating series, follow the journey of six remarkable boys as they navigate the tumultuous path of growing up without parents, discovering love, and finding their place in a challenging world.

Between Brothers (Book 0)- How it all began…
For Pete's Sake (Book 1)- Preston's story.
Crossing Jordan (Book 2)-Jordan's story.
Fire and Walter (Book 3)- Walter's story.
The Perfect Guy (Book 4)-Guy's Story.
The Patience of a Saint (Book 5)- Saint's Story.
A Case of Love (Book 6)- Case's Story.

The Pryce Sisters

Follow the remarkable journey of the Pryce triplets as they navigate the complexities of growing up, discovering romance, and embracing the exhilarating challenges of the new adult years.

Baby For A Pryce- Book 1
Right Pryce Wrong Time – Book 2
Yours, For A Pryce- Book 3

The Jacksons

Prepare to be enthralled by the captivating saga of the Jackson family. In this gripping series, secrets unravel, paternity questions loom, and love blooms in the most unexpected corners.

Ace- Book 1
Deuce- Book 2
Trey- Book 3
Quade- Book 4

The Scarlett Series

Their patriarch died and unexpectedly left each of them a fortune. Watch as the Scarlett family navigate their way through the ups and downs of sudden wealth, family secrets, and the complicated dynamics of their relationships.

Scarlett Baby (Book 1)
Scarlett Sinner (Book 2)
Scarlett Secret (Book 3)
Scarlett Love (Book 4)
Scarlett Promise (Book 5)
Scarlett Bride (Book 6)
Scarlett Heart (Book 7)

Magnolia Sisters

They were the rejects. The worst of the lot, they grew up in a girl's home together and formed sisterly bonds. Each book in the series tells the story of a different girl and the unique struggles and triumphs she faces along the way. With themes of friendship, forgiveness, and the power of love, the "Magnolia Sisters" series is a heartwarming and inspiring read that you won't want to put down.

Dear Mystery Guy- Book 1
Bad Girl Blues- Book 2
Her Mistaken Dream- Book 3
Just Like Yesterday – Book 4

New Song Series

A group of friends started out as a church band, see how each of them navigate their personal and professional lives while staying true to their faith and facing challenges along the way. With themes of forgiveness, redemption, and second chances, the New Song Series is a captivating read for anyone who enjoys heartwarming stories of love and faith.

Going Solo- Book 1
Duet on Fire- Book 2
Tangled Chords- Book 3
Broken Harmony- Book 4
A Past Refrain- Book 5
Perfect Melody- Book 6

The Bancrofts

The Bancroft family delves into the inner workings of academia and the high-stakes world of university politics. The family wrestles with the pressures of maintaining their family's legacy, they must confront their own demons and navigate the complex relationships that bind them together. From unexpected love affairs and betrayals to scandals and secrets that threaten to tear them apart, this is a series that will keep you captivated until the very end.

Homely Girl- Book 0
Saving Face- Book 1
Tattered Tiara- Book 2
Private Dancer- Book 3
Goodbye Lonely- Book 4
Practice Run- Book 5
Sense of Rumor- Book 6
A Younger Man- Book 7
Just To See Her- Book 8

Three Rivers Series

Three Rivers Series, a captivating tale of love, redemption, and second chances set in a picturesque community in St. Ann's Bay, Jamaica.

Private Sins- Book 1
Loving Mr. Wright- Book 2
Unholy Matrimony- Book 3
If It Ain't Broke- Book 4

The Resetter Series

The Resetter Series takes a look at a rare kind of person, a person who can travel back in time, but they only have one chance to get things right if they go back! With themes of second chances, changing the past and the power of love, the resetters series is a captivating time travel romance that many readers have described as a page turner.

Never Too Late- Book 1
Never Say Never- Book 2
Now or Never- Book 3
Almost Never- Book 4

On the Rebound Series

Experience the gripping and emotionally charged On the Rebound series, where love, betrayal, and redemption collide in a whirlwind of passion and secrets. Brace yourself for a journey filled with drama, cheating scandals, DNA questions, and ultimately, the power of second chances and finding love again.

On the Rebound- Book 1
On the Rebound Book 2

Standalone Books

Full Circle- After graduating from university, Diana wanted to return to Jamaica to find her siblings. What she didn't foresee was that she would meet Robert Cassidy and that both their pasts would be intertwined, and that disturbing questions would pop up about their parentage just when they were getting close.

After the End- Torn between two lovers. Colleen married her high school sweetheart, Isaiah, hoping that they would live happily ever after, but life intruded, and Isaiah disappeared at sea. She found work with the rich and handsome Enrique Lopez as a housekeeper and realized that she couldn't keep him at arm's length.

Love Triangle: Three Sides to the Story- George, the husband. Marie, the wife, and Karen-the mistress. They all get to tell their side of the story.

New Beginnings- Inner-city girl Geneva was offered an opportunity of a lifetime when she learned that her 'real' father was a wealthy man. Her decision to live up-town meant she had to leave Froggie, her 'ghetto don,' behind. She also found herself battling with her stepmother and battling her emotions for Justin, a suave up-towner.

The Preacher and the Prostitute- Prostitution and the clergy don't mix. Tell that to ex-prostitute Maribel, who finds herself in love with the Pastor at her church. Can an ex-prostitute and a pastor have a future together?

Historical Fiction

You won't want to miss out on these two captivating reads!

"The Pull of Freedom" tells the story of a slave family and their desperate struggle for freedom in Jamaica's colonial era. Follow the journey of these brave individuals as they fight for their right to be free, facing danger, heartbreak, and unimaginable obstacles along the way.

"The Empty Hammock" takes readers on a journey through time, as a modern woman finds herself transported back to the Taino era of Jamaica's history. Experience the wonder and mystery of this ancient culture through her eyes, as she learns about their traditions, beliefs, and way of life. With richly drawn characters and a beautifully realized setting, "The Empty Hammock" is a must-read for anyone who loves historical fiction that transports them to another time and place.

Short Story Collections

Di Taxi Ride and Other Stories- Funny stories about Jamaican life to make you laugh.

www.ingramcontent.com/pod-product-compliance
Lightning Source LLC
Chambersburg PA
CBHW050512160726
48003CB00001B/265